Digital Ps[...]

By Adam Colton

A Psychological Mystery

All contents of this digital book, Digital Psychosis, are copyright 2022 to Adam Colton

ISBN: 9798365646469

All rights reserved: no part of this publication may be reproduced, stored in a retrieval system, or transmitted, in any form or by any means, electronic, mechanical, photocopying or otherwise, without the prior consent of the author

Cover Design by Adam Colton

For more information on digital and physical copies of Adam Colton's books email hamcopublishing@aol.com

"All the world's a stage, and all the men and women are merely players"

- William Shakespeare (As You Like It)

Author's Note

This novel is intended as a melting pot of ideas.

Having written a novel about narcissism ('Codename: Narcissus'), I wanted to write about a combination of psychological conditions that seem somewhat related, namely *impostor syndrome* and *dissociative disorder*.

I think we all suffer from the former from time to time, having a sense that others are more qualified at life and feeling that we are merely acting the way we are expected to act and hopefully getting away with it. The central character, Steven, spends so much of his life acting that he completely loses himself. As for the latter condition, depersonalisation and derealisation respectively mean having a sense that either oneself or the world at large isn't real. These are facets of dissociation.

Toss in a well-meaning friend who thinks drugs might be the perfect answer to Steven's problems, as well as all the weirdness that the Internet can throw at somebody, and I think Steven will be in for a roller-coaster ride, as well as everybody else around him.

As with 'Codename: Narcissus,' this is a novel and not a diagnostic manual, and there is plenty of information about these conditions which can be found online.

Chapter 1 (Steven)

Laying on your back 24-7 can be a cure for some minds and a cancer for others. It all depends if your life is something that needs to be cured or if it is a finely-tuned engine of pleasure.

I suppose I had better introduce myself. My name is Steven Jones. It's a stupid name. Say it over and over again, go on, keep repeating it. It sounds stupid, right? And anyway, how can three syllables sum up what a person is, not just at this current moment in time but at all moments in time, forever? That's why I don't like names. How can you put a name on a person when a person isn't even the same from one year to the next?

Some people stabilise their egos by being proud of the place they're from. Imagine coming from London with all its history, Liverpool with its musical heritage or beautiful Bath. Well I live in a fairly anonymous town called Wickersby. It's OK but it doesn't seem to elicit much jealousy when I tell people where I'm from, which isn't often, as most people I seem to meet in Wickersby come from Wickersby. The town is bisected by a road called the A48 and there's an area of moorland that overlooks it, which is great if you like looking at heather. And no, I'm not being sarcastic, I love it up there.

So what am I doing laying here in bed?

Well, it's that stupid virus, right? Somebody decided it was a good idea to eat a bat and the whole world got plunged into catastrophe. I'm telling you now – it's not a good idea to eat a bat, or a pangolin, or whatever dumb creature it was that created this thing! Do you want to be lying on your back in a single room for weeks on end when you're supposed to be in your prime? No, didn't think so.

Huh, your prime – what does that mean? I'm 37. That's a prime number, right? But anyway, does calling this your prime mean if I'm not happy now I'll never be happy? Seriously, it was all uphill so far and if this is the peak, it must be downhill all the way until I meet the bloke with the scythe. No, I don't believe in all that 'in your prime' nonsense. You get good days and bad days and perhaps the good ones are more common at 37 than at 57 for most but it's just a statistic, and all statistics are just an average, aren't they?

My wife is called Anne. She's in her prime too. She's 35, but that's not a prime number. She's out at work at the mo, crunching numbers for Jessop and Davies Accountancy. Jessop still works there but Davies died a few years ago. He probably died of boredom.

I mean, does anybody actually *want* to be an accountant? Or is it just a job that people end up doing, like cleaning toilets? Anyway, Anne is treating me pretty well at the mo. She brings me meals all the while I'm Superglued to this bed by fate. She sleeps in the spare room at the moment, not that this is a radically different state of affairs to usual. Let's just say our marriage hasn't been passionate for a good year or more. She seems to like it this way. She prefers staring at columns of figures representing somebody else's money than paying attention to me these days. In short, she's a workaholic.

'What do I do?' I hear you ask. Well, when I'm not struck down by this poxy virus I'm an actor. Now, you might not consider my profession to be acting but it's what I do whenever I walk through those doors.

Alright, alright, I work in a pub called the Unicorn. I sometimes do the afternoon shift and I sometimes do the evening shift but it's not just bar work, it *is* acting. You see, I suffer from something called *impostor syndrome* which basically means that a lot of the time I feel less qualified at this whole 'life' thing than other people seem to be. It's like they all got the rule book written by Almighty God at birth and I got a pamphlet full of adverts.

Yes, that's a joke. You can laugh, but there's a serious point. Sometimes I wonder if I'm real and the others are all acting, but generally it seems the other way round, like I'm from another planet, sent to observe human life while attempting to assimilate with it. There's also a condition called *dissociation*. Google it. I wonder if I have that too.

Look, I'm going to be lying on my back for at least another week, so I might as well tell you my story. Things have got a bit weird lately so I've a lot to unravel. Let me get a cup of tea and then I'll be back to describe a typical day at the Unicorn pub in Wickersby. You'll soon get the point. Point – Unicorn - get it? Oh well, never mind...

Chapter 2 (Steven)

Right, I'm back. Let's just imagine a typical day at work. Are you ready? OK, here goes...

Panic.

I'm about to start the afternoon shift and I'm walking through the car park towards the back of the Unicorn. I feel like I am on rails, as though I am just being carried along, regardless of whether I want to be or not. It's a small square car park surrounded by green bushes. My heart pounds as the white plaster wall of the eighteenth century alehouse gets closer. I'm being swept towards it.

When I'm myself I enjoy this job, chatting to the locals as they drink their pints, having small talk with the barmaids, especially Anabelle. Annabelle is 22 and she has a boyfriend who I have never met. Aaron, I think his name is. I sometimes wish I was her age again. Her life is all ahead of her and there's a good chance that her and her boyfriend will make a go of it. You see, Anne and I have made a hash of our marriage, but isn't this what everyone does? And those who don't openly cock it up are just pretending it's all fine, right?

Allow me to elaborate. You have a thing called 'desire' which may be what people call 'love' or it may be what they call 'limerence,' but this is what gets two people together in the first place. Why? Well, humanity wouldn't exist if people didn't have babies, so the passions need to be strong. But hang on, the joke's on you, because as soon as you've been together long enough to produce a child or two, it has to die down. Why? Well, if every couple stayed wrapped up in each other they would be ignoring the needs of the babies, and then the babies wouldn't last very long. And that's no good for population growth. So you see, it can't be any other way. Except that Anne and I didn't have babies. She has her Microsoft Excel spreadsheets and I have 'The Good Beer Guide.'

So Anabelle? Yes, she's nice and she sometimes acts in a way that people call 'flirtatious,' but I think that this is an act too. It must be, as her boyfriend would knock the stuffing out of anyone else who came near her. Anabelle and I are both acting, except that I'm acting just to get through the day and she's having fun with her act. Sometimes it feels like I'm not a real person at all, like I'm just playing at it, like those hippies or punks who played at 'revolution' before signing their souls away to rampant capitalism. I'm playing at 'life' but what have I signed up for? Well, that's what I'm trying to work out while I lay flat on this bed.

Back to the Unicorn. The back door is open and I wander inside, feigning a casual demeanour. I can hear Jimmy and Terry in the kitchen messing around loudly. They are typical chefs, both in their early thirties. Shall I say *hello*? Yeah, I think I will. It should set up the pretence for today and hopefully I won't have to try so hard later.

I put my head around the kitchen door. These two men are in their chef's whites as usual, surrounded by silver kitchen surfaces. 'Greetings gents,' I say.

'Oh, hi Jonesy,' replies Jimmy as Terry coolly raises his hand in restrained acknowledgement.

I retract my head from around the door frame and the pots and pans begin to bang again. The banter cranks back into action, like a gramophone record that's been turned off beginning to rotate once more. I hear water running; they've forgotten about me already. Anyway, I think I got away with it. The impostor has entered the building as smoothly as Elvis would have left it. Didn't he once croon something about all the world being a stage?

There's a narrow corridor leading from the kitchen to the bar. This is the worst bit. I call it the Hallway to Hell. Hey, that could be a hit by an obsessive-compulsive rock band – OCDC. Oh well, never mind...

Once I appear in that doorway I'm locked in for the day. By now I'll have been spotted by staff and customers alike, so that's it, the show can't be stopped until home-time. Sometimes I have to fake a toilet break just to get out for a few minutes on my own in order to give my brain a break from the incessant acting. I can get away with five minutes or so once an hour, but anything more is pushing it. I just lock myself in the cubicle and breathe deeply. It seems to help, but then I have to go through the whole process of psyching up again before I walk back out.

As I near the entrance to the bar, the daylight shining through the windows becomes brighter, while the walls of the corridor change from dull to radiant. It really is like walking out on stage; the blinding lights, the audience waiting in anticipation, except I haven't really got an act. It's just me pretending to be *me*, and who wants to pay to see that?

I take a deep breath. Here we go, wait for the applause.

Anabelle is facing the wall, filling a shot glass with some whisky from an optic. If I was on the other side of the bar I'd gladly neck a few of those down, by which time I'd begin to blend in. Reality would absorb me and I'd see that I'm just like the rest of them really, but am I? Do those boozy old men ever think these things? Or do they just go home after they've had a skinful and watch other people acting on Emmerdale and Coronation Street?

'Greetings Anabelle,' I say cheerily, as I take off my coat.

'Oh, hi Steven. Can't believe it's so busy already.'

She's wearing a blue skirt and a white blouse. I don't know how somebody so young can have the confidence of a fifty-year-old but that's Anabelle. Well, I hope that's what it's like to be fifty anyway. I'm 37 and I'm still waiting for confidence to arrive. It's like a train that never comes. Standing on the platform, looking at the display, and with every minute that passes the arrival time goes up by two minutes, except we're talking years when it comes to waiting for confidence, or happiness, or any other metaphysical thing, aren't we? Forever the outsider, forever the impostor. I mean what do 37-year-old blokes *do?* I don't mean go to the pub, watch football, work out at the gym, etc., I mean what are we *supposed* to do? How are we supposed to act?

I hang up my long brown coat on a peg at the corner of the bar and rub my hands together as I walk to the front. It looks confident, like I know what I'm doing, like I know how to *be* a 37-year-old bloke.

An old man with broken teeth ambles towards me. Here we go...

'I'll have a pint of that there Scragglewort bitter,' he says through a voice that's seen sixty years of cigarette smoke.

'No problem,' I say, faking confidence adeptly. They say that if you fake it for long enough you become it. They say lots of stupid things!

I reach for a pint glass from the rack above my head and walk over to the pump, awkwardly stepping past Anabelle, who is rushing around as usual. I reach for the handpump and pull it towards me as the brown liquid splashes into the glass. Scragglewort, now that's a name. Steven Jones, no, that's not a name!

I let the beer settle on the bar and then put it back under the pump for one final pour before passing it to the pensioner.

'Good ale that,' he says.

'Yeah, brewed right here in Wickersby at Olde Mill Brewery. First produced in 1922 by John Scragg although the strength was reduced from 6% ABV to 4.8 in the nineties to appeal to more family-oriented drinkers.'

'You know your stuff, youngun,' says the old man, as I slide the ten pound note out from under his grubby fingers. You see, when I come out with stuff that I know about I feel better. Steven Jones, the 'real ale' expert!

As I return from the till with the old man's change he contorts his face into a smile, which is really just the movement of wrinkled skin. 'You ever done the brewery tour?' he asks.

'Yes,' I reply. No, no, that's not good enough, so I add, 'I did it with my wife before we were married. It's an interesting building. It would have been on the edge of the town in 1922 but now it's surrounded by houses.'

'Oh aye,' says the old man lowering the glass from his lips which are now adorned with a froth moustache, 'I'm even too young to remember *those* days.' He wipes his mouth on his sleeve. 'Nice chatting to you,' he says as he walks away to return to his round table by the window, taking his place in a shaft of sunlight that has made it through the frosted glass after being uninhibited for 93 million miles. Think about it. All that distance just to land on the table in front of an old man and illuminate a pint of Scragglewort.

Well, that's about it really. That's my job in a nutshell.

Where is gets awkward is when people I know come into the pub. It's like unrelated bits of my life that don't belong together rubbing against each other. Abrasion, yes, that's it. I mean, there's my home life and my work life, my social life and my inner life. You don't just throw them all into a bag together and mix them up, but that's what it's like when friends are having a good time and I have to serve them the drinks. In short, it's flaming awkward.

I have a friend I see quite often called Martin Wilson. Just a few syllables again, and no, they don't really tell you much about him either, and if you say them over and over again his name sounds just as daft. He's a nice guy, but he dabbles with the funny stuff a bit. You know, he snorts the old talcum powder stuff, smokes the odd jazz cigarette, takes pills that aren't in the pharmacy aisle in Tesco's, know what I mean?

Now, I often ask him why he needs it, but he says that *his* life is an act too, but not in the way that mine is. I suppose everyone is running from something, depression, anxiety, OCD, you name it. Martin just deals with it in a medically questionable way. Sometimes I see his dealer hanging around outside the pub. He wears a woolly hat even in the middle of summer. I suppose it's a kind of disguise. A bleeding hot one at that! I think he pushes all sorts of weird stuff on Martin, uses him as a bit of a guinea pig. Martin gets it cheap and then he gives the dealer an in-depth product review.

Today's review, 'I was smashed out of my head!' Yeah, right!

Well, it's up to him I suppose, but you do wonder what kind of things he's unwittingly funding by buying all those illicit substances. Anyway, he's alright to talk to over a pint so I try not to judge. He just doesn't think that deeply about where his money is going, but then does anyone?

He usually gets on all that wacky stuff when he goes home and thankfully I don't have to witness that. I'm back indoors lying next to my unconscious wife by then. But that won't be happening for a while because like I say, I've got this poxy virus, so I've got the whole double bed to myself. She's in the spare room.

Hey, I might even get some sleep!

Chapter 3 (Steven)

So that's a bit about my work life. I mentioned my inner life just now. Well, it's not very 'inner' if I parade it all over this book, but it's not much of a book if I don't, so I suppose I'll have to tell you a bit about that at some stage. For now, I just document most of it until I can work out what to do with the contents of my head. One brain, fully loaded, no user's manual.

So I write my thoughts down every day in these little black books. They're like diaries but less obvious-looking. I've heard that people have little black books for phone numbers, but mine are for thoughts.

'Why do you waste time writing that rubbish?' is like a stock phrase of Anne's, who you will recall is my seldom-seen wife. That phase is a bit like a keyboard shortcut. Press shift and the number one and she says 'Hello,' press shift and the number two and she says 'Why do you waste time writing that rubbish?' It all seems a bit robotic. Is *she* acting too?

Anne and Anabelle, hey? I bet you spotted that. You're right, it gets confusing, and if I accidentally call my wife 'Anabelle' she thinks I'm trading her in for a younger model. It's kind of flattering that she thinks that, but fifteen years would be a serious age gap, wouldn't it? 'Mind the gap,' as they say on the London Underground!

Now, I know a bit about the author who is ghost-writing this for me and I know the kind of thing he does in his books, so if you've read any of them you'll be forgiven for making some kind of weird conclusion that Anne and Anabelle are the same person at different ages, and that if I left my wife and got involved with the lovely young barmaid she would eventually turn into my wife and I'd be back where I started. But you don't need a sci-fi plot to see that this is exactly what would happen anyway. Remember what I said about relationships and what has to happen so that the parents focus on the children? Yes, they all end up moribund. OK, you remember. That's good; you're taking it in then.

Now, Anne and I met at the pub funnily enough. She was there for a Christmas meal with her colleagues from Jessop and Davies Accountancy. Yeah, a right barrel of laughs, hey? I was surprised to see a young woman drinking pints of real ale and it turned out that she was a bit of a connoisseur of craft beers. We got chatting and she was interested to hear my knowledge on the subject and I can tell you that that's as rare as dung from the proverbial rocking horse. Anne's friends went home but she stayed behind and we shared tasting notes. She started talking about a new microbrewery in the town centre, so I said that I'd have to visit it and she suggested that we both went there when I next had a free night. It was as simple as that.

But every relationship is an arc, and once you've had the upward curve and reached the top, you know what comes next – you slide all the way back down.

So the 'up' part was that we courted for three years, toured every brewery across the county, and found that the various brews lubricated the conversation sufficiently to create rapport, until we found ourselves on a roller-coaster that led one-way to marriage. The 'down' part was everything that followed, you know, grown up stuff, like paying bills and setting up a mortgage – all the stuff they never show in romantic films.

So here's how it is with us these days:

If I'm on a daytime shift we actually get to spend the latter part of the evening together, and that's usually about as romantic as a telegraph pole.

'Hi, how was your day at work?'

'Well, I spent all day totalling up the month end accounts. How was yours?'

'I had to pop out and get some new soap cubes for the men's urinals. It smelled foul in there today.'

Well, that's killed the romance.

And if I'm on an evening shift, Anne comes in from the office as I go out to work. When I get home at midnight, I have a few drinks to relax and I feel pretty normal for a bit. It's hard to believe but I actually forget about the whole *impostor syndrome* thing. Then it's off to bed and I wake up at the bottom of that ladder again, with another day in which to climb fruitlessly to the top. Snakes and ladders, yes, that's it. Life is a giant children's board game with a hundred squares that you are destined to land on again and again. Up and down, and in the words of the Pink Floyd song, 'In the end it's only round and round.'

It's the same every day, Anne goes off to work, power-dressed like an extra in Dynasty, and I potter about until it's time for me to get behind that confounded bar again. Life behind bars, get it? Well, it feels like a prison sometimes.

But how did it get like this? Our wedding day was perhaps the high point – in more ways than one, for we got married at a little church at the top of the hill that overlooks Wickersby – Saint Cecilia's. It's a lovely old stone building with a backdrop of rolling moors covered with heather. Out the front you can see right the way across Wickersby, with the square tower of the parish church of All Saints being the most noticeable structure, protruding from the myriad roofs of the town centre. It's a fantastic view and it seemed the perfect place to tie the knot. Anne looked amazing, almost like a film star, with her hair in a style that I'd never seen her wear before. Or since. Hey, did I even marry the right woman?

Anyway, after the service and the photographs, which couldn't help but be photogenic with all that great scenery around, we all trundled down the A48 and into the town for the reception at a pub called the Black Dog. I didn't want it to be held at my workplace obviously, and the pub wasn't the 'yuppie' place it is now. In fact the wedding breakfast was spot on, right down to the prawn cocktail starter.

I didn't know Martin in those days, in fact I didn't even have a best man. This made it easy as there was no chance of being embarrassed in a speech, and I guess a best man's speech is a perfect example of bits of your life which should remain separate being thrown together, courtesy of a single potentially humiliating monologue. For others this might result in mildly rosy cheeks; for me such a notion seemed like death itself. No, Anne and I just had a handful of relatives with us. I was still nervous as hell when I made my own speech and I knocked a glass of champagne off the table. Well, some people celebrate by smashing glasses so I guess I got away with it.

After this we jumped into married life with both feet and negotiated a mortgage on this house of ours. Anne crunched the figures, with all the glee that a dedicated accountant could muster, and we signed our lives away. It seemed that we could achieve anything. But a veil was slowly descending between us and once all the bustle of moving into our first home had died down, there was a sense of 'what next?' And as the sense of 'what next?' increased, so did my sense of not really living at all. Anne dived into her work and I, well, I just carried on going through the motions at the Unicorn, but with increasing unease about who I was and what I was supposed to do.

There's got to be a way out of this maze, but as always, is there a maze, or am *I* the maze? Maybe everybody else runs around in my mind, like insects crawling around beneath my skin, making me itch until I'm crazy with it? This life has to mean something, surely? But it just trundles along the same. There's never a glimpse of the master-plan. 'Never knowing.' That's the story of my life, and if I shuffle off this mortal coil before Anne I've said that I want that etched upon my gravestone, after all it sums up my life better than 'Steven Jones.' 'Don't be morbid,' she says. That's another stock phrase of hers - 'keyboard shortcut number three' if you like.

'I'm not being morbid,' I say, 'But if I can't make any sense of things while I'm alive, this should be my final word to the world, my customer review on *reality*.'

So now you have it, you know my work life and you know my home life. And what's the one thing that binds them? Well, I told you – never knowing – always acting. And if this virus does me in and I'm gone before this book gets out, pop down to All Saints Church in Wickersby and you'll probably find a stone with those words etched upon it. I've already spoken to the vicar and he said it will be fine.

I can hear her saying it now – 'Don't be morbid!'

Chapter 4

Anne was in the Hummingbird Coffee Shop with her colleagues, Catherine and Jane. This was an ironic name for their meeting place of choice as Anne didn't drink coffee. In fact she never had done. A nice cup of tea was all she required to revive her after a hard morning ploughing through the figures at Jessop and Davies Accountancy.

It was a nice bright little place and it did a top-notch cappuccino, which particularly appealed to Catherine, the oldest and most rotund of the three women. The walls were painted yellow and there were pictures of flowers by a local artist hanging on the walls. One was of a bluebell and another was a foxglove, but that's about as far as the three ladies' botanical knowledge went. It was also a convenient place for the threesome to spend their lunch hour, as it was just around the corner from the office.

The three of them were dressed in smart skirts and blouses and they divested their heavy overcoats over the backs of their chairs to begin one of their regular lunchtime 'hot drinks and gossip' sessions, which were a bit like the 'Loose Women' TV programme but without the pay. Or the guests.

Anne wasn't sure whether or not she should break a confidence, but she trusted these two colleagues, and with her parents living at the opposite end of the country there were few people she could really talk to.

Taking a slurp of English Breakfast tea and placing the large round cup into her saucer gravely, she began, 'I'm worried about Steven.'

Jane and Catherine each gave a conciliatory smile and it was Jane who broke the awkward silence, 'It's not Anabelle is it? I mean she's a bit of a looker, isn't she?'

'Oh no,' replied Anne, 'It's worse than that. I'm worried about his mental health. You see, he keeps these diaries. He locks them away in a plastic container under the bed – loads of these little black books.'

'Men!' exclaimed Catherine, 'They just can't be loyal.'

'No, it's really nothing like that,' pleaded Anne, 'They're not for names and numbers, they're for his personal thoughts. One day I was doing a bit of hoovering under the bed and I hit the container, bending the plastic. I slid the box out onto the mat and tried to push it back into shape so that he wouldn't notice, but instead the lid flew open. Well, there they were, staring me in the face, all his little black books.'

'And don't tell me, you decided to read one?' laughed Catherine, picking up her cup and slurping some froth from the top of her cappuccino.

'Yeah, I did,' admitted Anne, 'And you should see the stuff he writes in them. I'm worried, seriously. He goes on and on about not feeling real and that he must be some kind of impostor on this planet, acting out the role of himself for everyone's benefit. For *my* benefit.'

'He's never taken drugs has he?' Jane enquired respectfully.

'He's never mentioned it,' defended Anne, 'No, he's not that kind.'

'Who is?' said Jane, 'I used to have the odd funny cigarette when I was a teenager.'

Catherine and Anne looked shocked. 'Jane Mitchell!' exclaimed Catherine in mock disdain.

'He's not a teenager,' said Anne calmly and forcefully, 'He's a 37-year-old man and I think he's losing it.'

The smiles drained away from her two colleagues' faces.

'So what are you going to?' asked Jane, sounding serious.

'What can I do?' replied Anne rhetorically, 'I can't tell him I've been reading his personal ramblings; he'll go berserk.'

For a moment the three of them sat puzzling together in silence. This was broken by a tall young man as he placed a large plate with three baguettes upon it down onto their table.

'There we go, ladies. Is there anything else I can get for you?'

'No, that's fine, thanks,' smiled Catherine, 'We'd better get munching or Old Man Jessop will be whining at us when we get back.'

'So much for pathos,' thought Anne wistfully.

Chapter 5 (Steven)

Right, what's next? I've done *work life* and *home life*, I'm hanging back on *inner life*, so I'd better do *social life*. I haven't got one at the moment, being laid up like a beached whale until I shift this damn virus. I'm getting fed up to the back teeth with it now. Talk about dragging on. Anyway, I'll tell you about some of the times when I *did* have a social life.

Sometimes I meet my friend Martin for a drink. Remember him, Martin Wilson, the sherbet addict? Well, he's had his fair share of white powder if you know what I mean. We don't meet at the pub where I work. We go to the Black Dog usually, the place where I had my wedding reception. It's a change for me to be away from the Unicorn, but really it's not my kind of place these days. The thing is it's trying to be a yuppie dining establishment. The staff were chatty there once upon a time, but now as soon as anybody chats to you the manager comes out barking orders at them to wipe tables, collect glasses, or do anything apart from talk to the customers.

Martin is a few years older than me and he's *lived*. At least that's what he says. What he calls 'living' seems to exclusively involve taking mind-altering substances bought from a dodgy looking bloke who wears a woolly hat all year round. Seriously, Martin talks about what he's stuck up his nose, in his mouth and 'God knows where else' as though it's some kind of badge of honour. Some people boast about their holidays. You know, 'I've been to Florida, Switzerland and New Zealand,' but Martin's list of achievements is more like, 'I've done weed, I've done ecstasy, I've done acid...'

I suppose people have different ideas of what *living* means and sometimes I'd like to take a step out of my own mind and see what it's like to be somebody else, but not in that way. It would be nice just to have a break from all this acting. It would be nice not question my every move, to feel like I actually belong here as much as anybody else. But no, a few pints is fine for me. I'm not interested in seeing pink elephants coming out of my nostrils.

The only criticism I have of Martin is he's a bit shallow sometimes. As soon as I start talking about my philosophy of life he tries to lighten the tone. Huh, my philosophy of life! It makes it sound like I actually have one. What I mean is 'my attempts to make sense of this brief time on earth.'

I was talking about relationships to Martin one time. 'Things are going belly up with Anne I'm sure,' I said, 'But that's evolution.'

'Eh?' said Martin, 'What are you going on about?'

'Evolution, it's evil. The clue is in the name,' I interjected wittily while taking a sip of Cherry Tree Ale.

'Ha ha, like it. Evil-lution, yeah!'

I could tell that Martin wasn't ready for a deep conversation but I decided to give him one all the same, explaining my theory regarding the 'best before date' on relationships and how they have to be that way to enable the next generation to survive beyond infancy.

'Jesus, Steve!' exclaimed Martin, 'So you're pretty much saying all relationships are a trick just to get you to have kids.'

'That's exactly what I'm saying,' I said, surprising myself at the firmness of my response.

'Man, you really need a chill pill. Your brain is eating up all your energy, mate. And where's it getting you?'

'God knows,' I replied, exasperated, 'I'm going to the loo.'

'Have one for me too,' joked Martin, 'I can't be bothered to move!'

Unbeknown to me, while I am in the gents studying a humorous poster, Martin is up to some very murky business in the bar area. He pulls a white envelope out of his pocket and empties some kind of powder into my beer. He then picks up my glass and sloshes it around, trying to create a kind of centrifuge to mix in the mysterious additive. He accidentally sloshes some onto a beer mat and wipes it away meticulously with his sleeve, squaring up the glass so that it is in the same position that it was in when I left the room to drain the tank, as they say.

I return to the red-cushioned seat and I take a lug from my pint.

'It's got a funny flavour this ale,' I say, 'It's what I call *flowery*.'

'You mean like flour you make bread with?' says Martin. He's clearly got white powder on the brain.

'No, flowery as in *floral*. It's too sweet for me really.' Martin leans back in his seat, seeming more relaxed. 'I prefer hoppy flavours,' I add.

'Should've had a lager, mate,' quips Martin, who has never been into real ales, 'It's all like ditchwater that stuff.'

'Yes, but at least there are different varieties of ditchwater,' I state, 'That lager stuff is all the same.'

'It's all the same and it's all good,' dismisses Martin as he necks down the remainder of the amber fluid in his glass, 'Come on, it's nearly closing time.'

I sup the remainder of my pint in a few mouthfuls, smacking my lips as though trying to get my head around the strange flavour. I was sure it tasted better before I popped into the gents.

'That Cherry Tree Ale is a weird one,' I inform Martin, who was now looking at the bar. He clearly wasn't interested, but I decided to continue anyway, 'Oakbourne Brewery name all their seasonal ales after fruit. They've only just started doing this one.' By now Martin has retrieved my long brown coat from the hook on the wall and has draped it over my arm. No more tasting notes for tonight it seems, so I drink up, and throwing my coat around myself we acknowledge the barman and leave. Stepping outside, I notice an immediate chill in the air as the wind whips an empty chip paper along the pavement of the residential street.

'You're not working till evening tomorrow, are you?' asks Martin.

No, why?' is my response.

'Just wondered really. You've had a few so you might need some rest time.'

This seems a weird thing to say, as I drank no more than I usually do when I meet him.

'Well, I'll be walking down the Hallway to Hell at 6pm,' I quip.

'OCDC,' returns Martin; he's heard that joke of mine before. Then he adds, 'Well, you take it easy. Maybe don't drink any more when you get in tonight. See ya.'

'Yeah, right, see you,' I say slowly, feeling somewhat confused, and then the panic hit me. 'Did I seem drunk?' I wonder, 'Maybe I overdid it tonight and Martin didn't want me to look daft when I get in.'

The truth is, Anne has never really worried about me going out for a few pints, but then I've never come in in the state some blokes do. Suddenly, apprehension returns, as though the mellowing effect of the beer has dissipated in a moment. I would have to *act* once again. Normally I'm trying to act up my confidence, but when I got back I'd have to play it down. I'd have to be *less* confident than usual to avoid it seeming that I'd gone overboard at the pub. I mean, why was I feeling this way anyway?

As Martin and I walk away from the Black Dog in opposite

directions I concentrate on the streetlights, which are evenly placed along the dark suburban road, each filling the air around it with a little halo of garish orange light, as though stamped into the thick night air which covers everything like a velvet curtain.

I pass a white courier's van with the slogan 'Precise Deliveries' written on the back. I think to myself 'What a stupid phrase.' I mean, you wouldn't want a courier whose deliveries were imprecise, would you? For example, he's found your road so he delivers your prized package to one of your neighbours as their house number is quite similar to yours.

Then I wonder, 'How many streetlights have I passed since passing that van? I need to concentrate.'

I observe the metal poles gliding by as I pass each lamp; it seems as though I am speeding up. I pass one orange globe of light, then another, and another, but I can tell by the movement of my legs that I am not running. This is very confusing. The lights seem to be whipping past as though I am speeding down the road on a bike or something, but at the same time my legs are hardly moving at all as I consciously slow my movements down.

I begin to panic. I just want to be home, tucked up in bed. Am I actually running? Perhaps there's a reason that I am running. Is somebody chasing me? The lights are whipping past faster and faster, it's all becoming a bit of a blur. Oh God, I feel sick now. So I stop and I slump down on the pavement against a brick wall which is adorned with the obligatory graffiti.

'That's odd,' I think to myself, noticing that the wall is not decorated with the usual four-letter words or meaningless tags, but a long number. It has seven digits and it starts with a 'one,' so it must be a million and something. With my back against the wall I put my head between my legs. The sickness begins to subside and I collapse sideways onto the tarmac.

Now, this is not a standard night out and I realise that I've strayed from my original intention of illustrating an average night out with Martin, but it happened and the truth is, this incident became quite instrumental in investigating that fourth area of my existence that always seemed so bewildering to me:

– My inner life.

Chapter 6

The Hummingbird Coffee Shop was packed and the three women sat around their usual round table in the corner, trying to ignore the backs of the people crammed into all the available spaces around them.

'Can we be serious for a minute?' ventured Anne.

'Oh,' said Jane, putting her cup back in the saucer and pulling a mock serious expression.

'Do you remember what I said about Steven's little black books?'

'Of course,' said Catherine, 'Your husband is an avid diarist.'

'Well yeah, but I'm getting tempted to take another peak in one.'

'Ooh,' exclaimed Jane, dropping the funny expression, 'That's a bit disrespectful. I mean the first time it was an accident but a second time...? You're not suspicious of him, are you?'

'Not in that way, but I'm seriously wondering if he has been taking drugs now. I googled *impostor syndrome* after we met up last time. He mentions it a lot in his writing. I still don't understand what's going on in his head but I think something he is taking might be causing it.'

'What do you mean?' said Jane, 'Has something else happened to make you think this?'

'Well, the police brought him home last night. They found him slumped across the pavement by a Transit van.'

Silence.

'At 4am,' added Anne, hoping this would pique their interest.

'Could have had one drink too many,' said Jane.

'No, this is the weird bit. He said that he couldn't have been by the van as he'd been running for several minutes after passing it. Then he felt sick and keeled over by a brick wall. Now you can't tell me that this is the result of too many drinks. I think he's on something.'

'Did you confront him?' enquired Catherine.

'No, not yet, I mean how do I do that? He's not a teenager. He says someone must have spiked his drink, but come on, this is the Black Dog. It's not exactly a crack den.'

The other two ladies laughed, then Catherine folded her fingers together with her elbows on the table, 'So there's only one way to find out, right?'

Anne looked her in the eye and waited for her to elaborate.

'The diary!' stated Catherine in a loud booming tone, sounding like the voice-over on a film.

Anne looked up at the extractor fan pensively as though searching for divine guidance before lowering her head, as if now in possession of the necessary morals. 'If he puts all his thoughts in there he's bound to mention if he's taking something, even if he codes it in his writing somehow. But I just don't think I could go snooping around in his books. The other day I accidentally knocked his plastic box open and curiosity got the better of me. It was *spur of the moment*. To go rooting around in there premeditated just seems wrong.'

'Yeah, but is it?' tossed in Jane, 'If he's on drugs you might be able to help him, but if you don't know nobody can help at all.'

'Put it this way,' said Anne, 'Would you like it if your boyfriend started rummaging around in your handbag?'

'Finding a boyfriend would be a good start,' laughed Jane, holding up her left hand to illustrate this by the lack of a ring.

Catherine smiled, 'Men aren't interested in what's in a woman's handbag. Men are different to us. They're so devious, you've got to keep one step ahead.'

Catherine had had a lot of bad experiences with boyfriends which had led her to have a somewhat misandrist view of life. Her current boyfriend, Matt, was the first partner who had treated her well and Anne knew that he wouldn't stick around long if Catherine held onto such generalisations about his gender. No, Anne wasn't going to go poking around in Steven's private things. 'If a couple can't respect each other's boundaries then they shouldn't be together in the first place,' she stated, and with that she picked up her cup and slurped down the remainder of her tea as if swallowing away the unpleasant aspects of the conversation.

Then, strategically changing the subject, Anne announced, 'Old man Jessop's got the auditors coming in tomorrow.' Jane and Catherine groaned in unison. They hated having outsiders poking around in the accounts.

Chapter 7 (Steven)

I think what might be interesting now is to illustrate a time when my work life and my social life clash together; two different areas of my life grating away at each other like precious crystalware rattling around in a trolley. So where do we start? Well, this anecdote begins at work, and that only means one thing - panic time.

As ever I wander in via the small car park at the back of the Unicorn and take a deep breath. Here we go, another afternoon shift, another play that will go on for almost six hours, a play where I don't even know the character I'm playing. No instruction manual, remember?

I step out and look up to the sky. It's blue and there are some wood pigeons sitting on the apex roof. Their lives are simple. They never have to think 'Am I acting the way a wood pigeon is supposed to act?' They never wonder if other wood pigeons can see through their disguises.

'Hey, he did four coos instead of five just now. I don't think he's a real wood pigeon!'

I stroll towards the back door. I can hear Jimmy and Terry chatting in the kitchen already.

'How many times have I said *go easy on the garlic?* But no, she puts loads of it in anyway. I couldn't taste anything but garlic. It was terrible!'

I wander in the back door and stand in the kitchen doorway, waiting for a gap in the conversation to greet them, but they just continue.

"...So the next time she did it without any garlic at all. Well, that was no good whatsoever. She's got no idea of subtlety in the kitchen. It's all or nothing. That's why I wish she'd just let me do the cooking.'

Just then a saucepan goes flying past and lands perfectly in the large sink filled with soapy water. 'Oh, hello Jonesy,' says Jimmy, finally registering my presence.

'Hello,' I reply. Terry, as ever, raises his hand in a silent wave. It's weird how he's so chatty when it's just the two of them in that kitchen, but as soon as I walk in it's like his mouth's been taped up. 'Nice day,' I add, 'Sunny but cool.'

'Yeah,' agrees Jimmy, 'It's always roasting in here though. All that hot air that Terry comes out with.'

Huh, not when I'm around.

I laugh politely and steel myself for the Hallway to Hell. Am I going to keep up the act today? Is the mask going to slip? The thing is, I think the same thoughts every shift and somehow I always get through it, but still the uneasiness comes back daily, like the tide returning to the shore. As I come through to the front of the pub I notice Anabelle in a red dress. 'She's dressed up to the nines today,' I think, but the second thing I notice is Martin sitting on his own under that same stream of light that the old *Scragglewort* man had been sitting in the other day. 'This is going to be uncomfortable,' I surmise.

The thing is, a conversation I'd have with Martin is different to a conversation I'd have with Anabelle, or even old 'Misery Guts' who owns the Unicorn, but thankfully he's not often there. Why can't Martin see that turning up here out of the blue like that is going to seem odd? The problem is he gets quite loud and he frequently references what I'll politely call his 'experiments.' Should I laugh and joke with him, like I do when we're at the Black Dog, or should I remain coolly detached like a professional barman should, showing disapproval whenever illicit substances are mentioned? It's bad enough acting the part of myself, but today I've got to be some kind of hybrid of two different versions of myself, one adapted to my work life and the other adapted to my social life.

'Hi,' calls Anabelle across the bar, 'Your mate's popped in.'

'Hi,' I reply, 'I'd better go and see him before I get stuck into work. Are you OK for a few minutes?'

'Yeah fine,' says Anabelle.

'If only Anne could be as chilled out as she is,' I think to myself, but I guess that proves my point. It's all sweetness and light when you barely know someone, but as soon as you start living together, all that tolerance fades. Before you know it you might as well be married to Kim Jong-Un!

This is odd; Martin hasn't even noticed me. His eyes seem fixed upon the dust floating around in that sunbeam.

He turns to me, as if startled. 'Steve,' he exclaims, 'I owe you an apology.'

'Really?' I'm racking my brain but I can't for the life of me think of any time that we've ever fallen out.

'Sit down a mo. I've checked that Anabelle's OK with it. I need to tell you something.'

'Oh gosh, this sounds serious,' I think as I pull out one of the wooden seats and join him at the table. I gaze around. Is anybody looking at me? Is anybody within earshot of our conversation?

'I'm not staying long, but I had to see you,' Martin begins, 'You know you're always going on about this *impostor syndrome* thing you get? And how nervous everything makes you? Well, I just wanted to relax you a bit. I wanted to show you a different way.'

I nod, but I still haven't got a clue what he's talking about.

'I wanted to teach your brain new tricks, so to speak. Look, I'm sorry, I slipped something into your drink last time we were out.'

I laugh nervously, 'What like Viagra or something?'

Martin smiles, 'No, you can buy Viagra yourself if you want it. This was special stuff. I'm not even sure what it was. *Woolly Hat* palmed it off on me and it chilled me right out so I took a bit of a liberty. Look, I know it was wrong and I'm sorry. I've never done it before and I won't do it again.'

I'm still processing the information. Oh my god – the streetlights, feeling sick, getting in at 4am – he's on about that – he drugged me! My smile dissipates, as though pulled down by gravity.

'What the *hell* were you thinking of?' I whisper angrily, 'I could have been arrested. I thought I was running miles up the road and all the while I was laying unconscious by a white van.'

'Sounds about right,' said Martin, 'It's like time expands or something when you take it. Or maybe all times are linked and it makes us perceive things as they really are. I thought it might give you a different perspective and snap you out of that whole dissociative thing you get.'

'Well, thanks Doctor Kildare,' I remonstrate, 'But I'm not up for being a guinea pig in your psychological experiments.'

'Got it!' stated Martin, raising his hands, 'We've been meeting up for a couple of years now and I don't want this to mess things up. It was a *spur of the moment* thing. You went for a leak and I just thought *what the hell*.'

I'm lost for words, although admittedly I was so angry that I actually forgot about playing the part of myself and I felt comfortable, just for a moment.

'Do you want to know what happened to me when I took that stuff?' ventured Martin.

'Not really, but I expect you're going to tell me.'

'I had a revelation. I was laying in bed and the room seemed to be bathed in all this light. Weird supernatural light. And I could see a figure on the wall. It wasn't scary and I felt totally calm.'

I pulled a sceptical face but Martin knew what I was thinking, 'No, not like a silhouette, I mean a number, a *numerical* figure. The number must have meant something as it was so vivid.'

'What was it?' I asked.

Martin flicked over a beer mat and on the underside he had written '1048576.'

'Oh wow,' I gasped, 'Two to the power of twenty.'

'Eh?' said Martin.

'It's binary,' I explained, but Martin just looked confused, 'Computers work on a binary system. A kilobyte never used to be a thousand bytes but a thousand and twenty four – two to the power of ten. Now what do you think you get if you square a thousand and twenty four?'

Martin looked at me mysteriously and then looked at the beer mat, before slowly reading the number he'd written on it earlier.

'Exactly,' I said, 'Now, with your F-grade in GCSE maths, don't you find it strange that a significant number like that would come to you in a drug-addled stupor?'

'Alright mate,' defended Martin, 'There's no need to be like that.'

I cast my mind back to my own hallucination, or whatever it was. There was a number scrawled on the wall and it could have been the very same figure. It was definitely a million and something.

'Seriously,' I said, 'This is interesting. I saw a number too when you foisted that stuff on me and I think it was probably the same. Let me think.' For once Martin is quiet. 'Let's say something from beyond this world was trying to communicate with us. It wouldn't understand our language, but one language is the same wherever you go – the language of maths.

'You see,' I continue, 'That number will be significant to any civilisation in the universe. I don't believe it would arise out of sheer coincidence.'

'Man, that's crazy. Are you telling me that a few grams of this powder enables us to communicate with aliens?'

'I'm not sure what it means but the choice of that number indicates intelligence. It's like this particular drug opens up the mind to some sort of communication. We need to find out more, so maybe *you* can be the guinea pig this time. You seem to like taking the stuff, so let's see what else your brain can cook up for us while you're under the influence.'

'No, no, no,' Martin reasoned slowly, 'Look, what I did was a bad thing, a mistake. I shouldn't have done it to a mate, but this isn't the way to get even. I'm not going to get that stuff again. If *Woolly Hat* wants any feedback from me it's two stars out of five. Yeah, it chilled me out, but us both seeing the same number is freaky. Maybe you are right and it lets aliens or something communicate with us. Well, blow that for a game of darts, I'm out!'

I gaze across to the clock behind the bar. Now, if any kid is thinking of trying drugs I reckon listening to some of the stuff Martin comes out with would put him off for life. Or *her*, of course. Let's not be sexist here. Perhaps they could wheel Martin into schools and let him spout gibberish at assemblies. That would put the kids off for sure.

The big hand was approaching the twelve, indicating the start of my shift. I couldn't really let Anabelle run around serving all the customers on her own any longer. I'd remember Martin's hallucinatory number easily, but now I just needed to know what on earth to do with it.

'Look, I've got to start work now. It's not fair to let Anabelle run the place on her own.'

'Of course, mate. I just wanted to fill you in on what I did in case you were freaked out.'

'Well,' I replied, 'Not as much as I am now but I guess we're both in the same boat.'

'And it's sinking!' joked Martin.

I smile, 'I'll see you later in the week. Hopefully I'll have some ideas about that number then.'

'Yeah, I'll see you, pal, and like I say, sorry for my little experiment.'

'Apology accepted.'

I returned to the bar, confused but feeling different to usual. After serving lagers to a group of young men and a whisky to a smartly dressed businessman with a briefcase I noticed that Martin had left and all that remained was his empty glass on the table, now in shadow as the sun had moved around. I had forgotten about being the impostor and I had forgotten about acting; I had something else to think about now – a mystery – a project.

Chapter 8

The next time the three women met for lunch they ordered a selection of cream cakes which came on a silver tray. Catherine, being larger and older than her two colleagues, always thought of such additions to their usual hot drinks and baguettes as a guilty pleasure, but everybody needs some kind of pleasure after all – some kind of release, especially after spending all morning hunched in front of a screen analysing columns of figures.

After all the hustle and bustle of ordering their drinks and putting their outer garments over the backs of their chairs they settled down for the usual chat, holding their cups in their hands to feel soothed by the warmth.

'So Anne,' began Catherine as though she was chairing a meeting, 'Did you snoop?'

'Excuse me,' replied Anne, placing her cup back on the saucer and feigning mock outrage, 'What kind of wife do you think I am?' Then after a disappointed silence she quietly said, 'Yes, I did.'

Catherine leaned in while Jane took a bite out of a cream cake, splattering blobs of cream onto the plate in front of her. Anne placed her phone on the table and the two ladies looked at the screen.

'Friday March 11th. Snoozed until 10am. Watched BBC news over coffee and walked to the wall where I'd passed out. No sign of the graffiti I saw in that dream or whatever it was. If the messages come through hallucinations and Martin and I saw the same number then it has to mean something. But why two to the power of twenty? Why was this number in both of our hallucinations? Had pasty for lunch warmed up in...'

Jane reached out her finger to scroll up the text on the screen but Anne chipped in, 'There isn't any more, it's a photograph of his diary; you can't scroll a photograph.'

'You're being negative.' said Jane, but nobody seemed to get the pun.

'Seriously,' stated Anne, 'You can't tell me Steven's not taking something dodgy now?'

'Well, he only said he had a dream,' defended Jane, who had always had a soft spot for her friend's partner, 'A dream is a kind of a hallucination, isn't it?'

'I'm not sure,' Catherine chipped in, 'Two blokes having hallucinations. It sounds like the pair of them are dabbling to me.'

'Half the country is dabbling,' chipped in the ever-open-minded Jane, 'I mean there's a big difference between a funny fag and injecting heroin.'

'Well, I don't like it,' said Anne sternly, 'I wanted to find the entry for the night the police brought him home at 4am but it must be in a previous book. He came home while I was searching through his box so I had to slam the books back inside and pretend I was sleeping.'

'I think you should try to find it,' posed Catherine mischievously, 'Just don't get caught.'

'I still don't think it's right for me to spy on him like this,' mused Anne guiltily as she took a large bite out of a jam and cream horn, 'My heart was beating like a techno record last time.'

The ladies chuckled and Jane, the youngest of the threesome, joked, 'You're showing your age there. Nobody listens to techno these days.' Then she thoughtfully added, 'Do you not find it weird that you two sit here trying to work out what your blokes are up to while they probably do exactly the same with us down the boozer?'

'You think men gossip about us?' questioned Catherine, taking a slurp of coffee, 'Can't see it. They're not even curious about what us ladies get up to. My Matt is too busy thinking about that bleeding car of his.'

'There is another aspect to this mystery,' Anne butted in, picking up her phone. 'What do you think *that* means?' she added, putting it back down on the table to display another image from Steven's diary.

'It's just a number,' said Jane, 'And not even an interesting one like a phone number. No phone number starts with a one.'

'Add up all the figures,' suggested Catherine, wiping the pastry crumbs from her lips.

'Already done it,' announced Anne proudly, 'Thirty one. That's how old I was when we got married.'

'Ah, it's a coded message to buy you an anniversary present,' came the retort.

'Don't be daft!' countered Anne, 'He wouldn't come up with anything as convoluted as that. A code should be easier to remember than the thing you're trying to remember, not the other way round!'

'Look you dum-dums,' said Jane, slamming her cup into the

saucer clumsily, 'He mentioned two to the power of twenty in the diary extract. That's got to be what that number is. He's puzzling about it himself, remember?'

'Cripes, you're a genius!' exclaimed Anne, 'So do you think they're taking LSD or something to try to find the meaning of life but all they're getting is numbers?'

'Goodness knows!' scoffed Catherine, 'But whatever is going on, they're going to end up basket cases if they keep doing it. Seriously Anne, you've got to nip this in the bud. *Mid-life crisis* they call it.'

'He's only 37,' defended Anne.

'I'm sorry Anne, but he won't make 38 if he carries on like that,' stated Catherine.

'Ouch!' mocked Jane, ever-keen to tamp down the more sarcastic aspects of the older woman's conversation when directed at her sensitive colleague. 'Look, we'd better drink up. It's nearly two.'

Chapter 9 (Steven)

So are you ready for the journey into the inner sanctum now?

I've told you about my work life, my home life and my social life, but we're about to open up a hornet's nest. The inner life is like the nine-tenths of the iceberg below the water that you can't see.

Now, I mentioned once before that the bloke who is ghost-writing this for me usually writes psychological sci-fi. I get a lot of time on my own before I go to work so I've read a few of his books. One of his was all about putting silicon chips in people's brains, but it's not so odd is it really? Our brains are like miniature computers, constantly trying to find some kind of meaning within the series of random events we call 'life.' Our brains create little stories for us in order to give our lives a sense of direction. But as with a laptop, if you put garbage in you get garbage out.

That said, I prefer my silicon chips where they belong – in a computer. When I'm not reading obscure novels by even more obscure authors I pass the time in our study, surfing the wave of indifference known as the Internet. I sneak along to the study occasionally. Anne seems to think I've got to stay in this bedroom all the while I'm contagious but it's maddening. All I can say is *cobblers to that*! I'm trying to solve a nagging conundrum here and it all started with that seven-digit number – two to the power of twenty.

I must admit that the online world just frustrates me. I mean, look at it logically, there's Facebook, Instagram, Twitter, that weird Chinese one, and people think they have friends, but everybody seems to be posting stuff about themselves and only a few people seem interested in reading anything. It's like idiots shouting into a vacuum! And now that I'm laid up with this virus, how many of those so-called friends have bothered to ask how I am? How many even know that I've got the dreaded lurgy? As I said – indifference.

This feels like a glimpse of what it must be like to be dead. Just sitting here, marooned, and nobody really giving a monkey's. Seriously, when the country was in lockdown there was a bit of British community spirit, everybody making an effort to keep in touch and support each other. Now that I've actually got the poxy virus, I hear absolutely nothing from anyone, not even Martin. Although knowing the state he gets into, I doubt he can even operate a computer.

Now, our house is only a modest semi-detached property. We

were lucky to get a mortgage really. I've heard that you need to own a gold mine to rent a shed these days. Huh, and people say that this country is well-run! Well, here's a clue, everybody needs a house and if houses are stupidly priced then it's not well-run, is it?

Anyway, I've always viewed it that it was something of a coup to have a designated study in such a small property. It gives me a feeling of being in a house where I actually want to live rather than just being dictated to by financial necessity. That's what we live in – a financial dictatorship. We call it freedom but the dictator is not a human – it's money, and how much of that you have depends on how much you're prepared to live a lie and pretend that you like doing things society's way. When you think about it, everybody is acting; it's just that *I'm* actually aware of doing it.

Now, I like it in my study. It's a long thin room with the computer desk along one side and just enough room to squeeze past the swivel chair to get to the window, which looks out over a lovely magnolia bush. It's lovely for about a month and a half every spring at least.

There is a picture of some majestic-looking cliffs on the wall and a patterned rug between the computer desk and the window. The room is often quite dark but I prefer to let the natural light suffice rather than turning the lights on. There's a *cost of living* crisis you know. *Well-run*, my foot!

Well, it was a few days after that meeting in the pub with Martin that I was ruminating over recent events and I wondered ' What would come up if I typed that seven-digit figure into a search engine?' I remember tapping my teeth with the end of a pencil apprehensively before making the decision to type.

However, hitting 'return' revealed nothing more significant than what I already knew, specifically that the number was two to the power of twenty and that it now represents a *mebibyte* and not a *megabyte* of information, dispelling a common misconception, well, common among those who are curious about maths at least. There was also some mumbo-jumbo about it having some kind of deeper psychological meaning, being the number of change or something. People's brains will latch on to anything in their quest for meaning. Little stories, remember?

Just then an idea came to me. I wondered if anybody had used this figure as a domain name for a website, so I tried a few out, typing in the number followed 'dot com,' 'dot net' and a few other suffixes. It seemed that this was not a popular domain name, as there were plenty of opportunities for me to purchase the web addresses for myself. So I tried some more; 'dot info,' 'dot org,' etc.

'What about *dot gov*?' I thought.

I answered myself, 'No, don't be silly, it won't be a government website' but I typed in the suffix anyway. The funny thing was, I was distracted by a noisy pigeon flying past the open window and my left hand slipped as I typed, making it come out as 'dot grav.' Well, who's ever heard of a 'dot grav' web address? Yet bizarrely, I found that I'd struck gold. Well, actually I struck red, as this brought up a vivid magenta screen containing a box to type in an email address and another box below in which to submit a question. Any question.

'That's weird,' I thought to myself, as there was nothing on the page to indicate who the question was being directed to or what the purpose of the site actually was. I took a sip of coffee to delay my inevitable participation, before letting out a sigh and muttering 'It's now or never' while typing in my own email address.

'And the question...?' I mused, What would I ask a total stranger with a web address that Martin and I seemed to have been led to by hallucinations?

Another sip of coffee.

In the end I typed in the only question that came into my head and hit return. The question was 'Am I real?'

I picked up the coffee mug and wandered over to the small window. My coffee mug has a mathematical joke on it, 'Easy as 3.1415926...' with the numbers getting smaller and smaller as they run around the mug, implying that pi goes on forever, which indeed it does when expressed in decimals. This is known as an irrational number, but you knew that, didn't you?

It had started to rain and I felt rather foolish at having just typed a deep existential question into an anonymous website. I closed the window, and the spatters on the glass seemed to have a tranquillising effect as the small drops coalesced into larger drops as they slid down the pane. Sometimes my mind runs riot and I wondered if by typing in that question I had set in motion a chain of events that would have a life-changing effect. But then again, I have generally found that nothing has a life-changing effect. Not even marrying Anne. Day after day, year after year, I'm still puzzling over the same conundrums, with life seeming like a tedious version of 'The Da Vinci Code,' where every question leads to another puzzle to solve.

My thoughts were distracted by the familiar sound of an email plopping into the inbox on the computer. I wandered back across the gaudily patterned rug and became immediately confused, for the message appeared to come from my own email address. I sat down upon the swivelling office chair and clicked it open upon. What came up next was just insane:

'You are indeed real, because I am real and I am you.'

'This has got to be some kind of trick,' I thought to myself. Scammers will try anything to gain your confidence but this was a new one. I hovered the cursor over the sender's email address to see if they had used my own address to disguise their real identity, but it appeared that there was no gobbledygook web address underneath my own.

'Who are you?' I typed in response, before deleting the words and rephrasing my reply; if I wanted to get information it was best not to get the sender's back up.

'Kindly prove that you and me are one and the same.' Return.

I picked up the pencil and began tapping it restlessly on the keyboard while staring vacantly across the rug to the grey skies beyond the spattered window pane. 'A watched pot never boils,' I thought, knowing that I was effectively paralysed until another response came through. But I didn't have to wait very long. Another email, again seemingly from my own address, popped up on the screen:

'I will send an email to you at exactly midday. Do not open it until tomorrow. Do not change your routine in the meantime. This is very important.'

I was somewhat miffed by this, for I would now have to wait until morning to get any closer to unravelling the mystery. If I got up early to open the email this would constitute changing my routine and I didn't want to jeopardise this experiment, or whatever it was, by defying the instructions. 'I suppose it's got to be the usual thing then,' I reluctantly thought to myself, 'Early lunch, go to the pub for the afternoon shift, try to act normal, come home, have dinner with Anne (if she's home), kill time, write today's diary entry and go to bed.' Humdrum days.

Chapter 10 (Steven)

I checked my emails before going to bed that night, and as expected there was one that seemed to be from myself, which had been received at exactly midday. 'High noon,' I thought dramatically, before musing that every noon was probably 'high noon' for Martin. Actually, that's not fair, he's not a morning addict, it's usually in the evening that he lives the *high life*.

I remembered the instructions not to open the email and to keep to my routine, so I opened the bedside table and pulled out one of my little black books. 'I suppose I'd better do today's write-up,' I thought to myself. At times I wonder why I persist in documenting a life that is often dull and repetitive, but then if future generations want an accurate representation of what ordinary lives were like at the start of the twenty-first century it won't do them any good to read the diaries of the rich and famous, will it?

Anne was already asleep and in the early days of marriage I used to take my books elsewhere to do my daily review on life, for fear of waking her up, but it soon became apparent that it takes more than a small table lamp and the sound of a pen scribbling onto paper to disturb her slumber. She's probably deep in a dreamworld of ledgers and spreadsheets.

Ten minutes later I flicked off the lamp, but sleep came very slowly, as I speculated upon what might be revealed in the mysterious email the next day. In truth, I still thought the whole thing was some kind of elaborate trick. Was it just coincidence that the one website I'd found relating to the number in Martin's hallucination, and probably mine too, seemed sadistically designed to mess my head up even more? There must be a limit to how much a human brain can be expected to process?

I then gazed across at Anne and felt a wave of sadness wash over me, like the tide lapping the shore. She was asleep, facing out of the bed, breathing rhythmically and deeply, so close and yet so unfathomable. The early days of romance are long gone and our relationship is merely perfunctory now, as we pass each other in the house with little to say before heading off to our jobs at different times, like ships that pass in the night. The evening meal is really the only remnant of my original concept of marriage and if I'm on the evening shift at the Unicorn, this doesn't even take place.

The whole matrimonial experience now seems like an

expensively wrapped empty box. Of course, you are supposed to provide your own gift – a child – but if like myself and Anne you have chosen not to have one or those screaming balls of life, the box remains empty, with the romance slowly fading, or merely being swept aside by mundane functionality.

I can hear her saying it now, 'Don't be morbid!'

Observing the tangled weave of hair wrapped around the head on the pillow next to me, it often strikes me that the contents of every individual brain can never be known. Each mind is an independent universe, cut off from every other mind, and more to the point, cut off from the real world. In more romantic times in a half-asleep state I used to imagine that Anne and I could communicate with each other in thoughts, but now we barely communicate at all. Forget telepathy; a proper conversation would be a start!

No, the biggest delusion of all is that the contents of one's own brain are in any way connected with what happens in the real world. Now, I've never been a religious man, but perhaps prayer is something of a necessity – a way for humans to believe that their thoughts can have an impact on actual events – a way to feel that there is a connection between our own inner universes and reality. I don't fall for those tricks.

Well, all that conjecture seemed to divert my thoughts sufficiently for me to forget about the mystery email, giving sleep a foothold, until it could creep in fully and tranquillise an ever-churning mind. Sleep was bliss, and as always, it involved a journey into a parallel universe – the world of dreams.

"Anne and I had two children, both girls, aged nine and six. The older one was called Catherine and the younger one was called Jane. I didn't question why we'd named our offspring after Anne's work colleagues, or even the fact that we had children at all. It was as though I had been away for a long time and that I'd just forgotten this fact.

Anne had popped out and left me with them but I was getting increasingly tense. The younger girl was screaming and I banged my fist down onto the table to try to shock her out of it. Meanwhile the older daughter was relentlessly asking questions. Then suddenly I just flipped. There were four wooden dining chairs and I picked them up, smashing them down so that the legs broke off, but the children just laughed and found this funny, enraging me even more.

I was out of control, pulling down bookcases, flipping tables over and breaking everything that I could get my hands on. But then I surveyed the chaos around me and I felt terrible to have destroyed my happy home. I was supposed to be the adult here and I'd failed. What's more Anne would be coming back soon. She'd see the mess and she would almost certainly want a divorce.

I piled up all the debris in the middle of the room but I decided to rescue the books, imagining them as something sacred, the representation of knowledge, so one by one I plucked them from the chaos and piled them neatly against the wall at the side of the room. Staring at the pile of fragmented limbs from the wooden chairs and tables I wondered if I could salvage any of it. I needed Superglue.

I then found myself in the little local shop in the square at the end of our road – Millbrook Stores. I was looking for adhesive to fix the legs back onto those dining chairs. Then I'd try to sort out the rest of the mess. But the shelves in the store were like the walls of a maze as I followed the aisles between them, looking up and down the rows of groceries. I remembered that glue is usually kept behind the counter, so I just needed to find my way out of the maze and get to the till. But the labyrinth went on. I kept turning at right-angles as the shelves guided my route, only to find yet more aisles of colourful boxes, strategically positioned to entice the browsing shopper. Time was running out, if I ended up spending hours just trying to locate the till I'd never get back in time to glue everything back together before Anne came home. My marriage would be wrecked.

At last I found it. Behind the counter was a sour-faced woman in her sixties with curly permed hair, dyed an unnatural shade of brown.

'Do you have any Superglue?' I asked.

'I'll need to see your passport,' replied the woman, 'It's an age-restricted product.'

Luckily I had my passport with me. I reached into the back pocket of my trousers and pulled it out, flicking it open in front of her. She scowled, 'I'm sorry, but this doesn't really help me.'

I looked down at the passport photo – it was just a blank white square!

'There was a photo,' I said, 'But somehow it got removed.'

'Do you have a driving licence?'

'Not with me, no.'

Just then my mobile phone rang. It was Anne. I knew she'd got home and things were going to go badly wrong. Just who had been looking after the children while I was in the shop all that time? Had they injured themselves on all the debris from my blind rage. I needed to find out straight away but when I pressed the green button to take the call nothing happened. It just carried on ringing.

I pressed it again. Still nothing, so I gave it to the woman behind the till, 'Could you answer this please. I've forgotten how to use it.'

'I'm sorry but I'm not authorised to do that without ID.'

My brain wasn't working properly. I snatched the phone back and somehow it had connected to Anne. 'Come quickly,' she said, 'The house is on fire.' I pictured plumes of smoke billowing out of the windows of our semi-detached house. It was a horrendous mental image; my entire life going up in smoke. Before I could reply, a message came over the Tannoy system but it wasn't the kind of message you would get in a shop. It sounded more like a bored announcer on a railway station, lifelessly listing off a line of station names. The last one was my own name. 'I am a place, not a person,' I thought."

I woke up with a start, wondering what on earth had prompted my mind to come up with such a dream – fire and fury. People don't take much notice of dreams these days, but they seem endlessly fascinating at times when life seems bland. In a way I can understand Martin's fascination with illicit substances. For him they represent a desire to escape, but having now experienced this unwittingly for myself, I am even more sure that this is not the kind of escape I need. The experience has only added further questions onto the questions that I already had.

No, dreams are simpler. The brain just accepts the strange things that happen in dreams just as a child accepts its life. The dreaming mind doesn't question why a familiar place is not as it is in reality, or why a character in a dream can be one person one minute and somebody completely different the next. It doesn't ponder as to why seemingly unfunny things make us laugh and seemingly benign things petrify us. Dreams are life perceived with no mental filter, in a raw state, if you like.

When I woke again it was morning and I can vividly remember watching a gradually widening beam of light streaming in around the side of the curtains and wishing that I could return to the world of dreams, but not *that* dream. No, that was just disturbing.

As is the routine, Anne was up first, dressing hurriedly for another day of number-crunching for Jessop and Davies. I could hear her pottering around downstairs as I tried to snooze. 'Don't change the routine,' I thought to myself, remembering the instructions in the email.

Eventually I heard the front door slam and I knew that I was alone in the house. So what's the routine? Get up, shower, eat breakfast, fire up the computer, check my emails... This was exactly what I had to do.

However, the hamster had begun pacing in the wheel of my mind already. Just what would the previous day's midday email reveal? Once I'd made it down to the kitchen I plunged the lever down on the toaster and scooped some instant coffee into my cup, just as I always do. I never look inside the square coffee tin, but today I did. It looked strange, for in among the brown granules were small white grains.

'Surely Anne hasn't put coffee in the sugar tin?' I muttered to myself, 'I know she doesn't drink the stuff but come on!' Still, it tasted OK and if there was sugar in it I couldn't detect it, so I buttered my toast, trying to suppress the curiosity that was building inside me like a huge tidal wave. In the end I couldn't hold it back any longer; I took the plate and the cup up to the study and switched on the socket and the computer.

I remember being impatient, muttering 'Come on, come on' with a mouthful of toast, 'Damn Stone Age computer!'

I tried to distract myself by recalling the dream from the night before. I remembered something about a shop and Superglue, but by then the desktop came up on the screen and I opened up my internet browser, eventually locating my emails, and there is was, waiting to be devoured, one email received at midday on March 17th seemingly from my own email address. Pull the other one, mate!

I tried to delay the moment of truth by taking a swig of coffee and calmly placing the cup and the plate on the desk. Gazing at the window, I noticed that it was a brighter day and that the first traces of blossom had appeared on the magnolia bush outside. 'Who am I trying to fool with these delaying tactics? Here goes,' I declared, double-clicking the email.

'Thursday March 17th. Got up at 9am. Wet day. Tried putting

the .... .umber into my search .... a domain name and eve........ ....d a red web page in............. to ask questions. The rep.............. to come from my ....unt although this is imp..........d salad and a pork p............ and walked to work. Awful shif.. Nobody wanted to chat .bout th.. ..les and there were no familiar fa...s. Annabelle seemed a bit flirty. She knows I'm married, and she's too young to be interested, surely? Anne cooked spag bol for dinner. Martin wasn't up for a drink so I stayed in watching a documentary on climate change. Another email awaits but I can't open it until tomorrow. Those are the rules apparently.'

The words were exactly what I had scrawled in my little black book before turning out the lamp the night before. Immediately I concluded that it had to be a trick of some kind. Was a mind-illusionist like TV's Derren Brown behind this?

'Somebody is spying on me. And it's not funny,' I thought, 'If Anne logs onto the computer and sees comments like that about Anabelle she'll think something's going on.' This was beginning to seem more like a chess game with a mystery opponent.

My mind raced. Anne was the only person who had been in the house and how could she send an email containing a diary entry before I'd even written it? No, it couldn't have been her, but what should my next response be? It was too late to bail out and stop playing the game now as my interest had been piqued, and once that happens a course of action has to be followed through to its natural conclusion.

I began to type a response, eventually settling upon the simple question, 'How did you do that?'

Then it was back to the waiting game. I scoffed down the rest of the toast and knocked back the remaining coffee, trying to relax myself in the springlike glow of the morning which seemed so different to the day before. 'Waiting, waiting, waiting,' I murmured to myself like a mantra while pacing backwards and forwards from the desk to the window, pounding across that patterned rug. Then finally another email arrived and I sprung back to the desk like a coiled whip. I braced myself for another mind explosion and clicked open the email.

'*As I said before, I am you. I am future-you. I still have my diaries so I can just copy what I've written on a particular day.*

Surely this is sufficient proof? The website allows communication between two people as long as they are the same person at different times.'

It was the craziest thing I'd ever heard and I didn't believe it for one minute. The bloke must have watched 'Back to the Future' one time too many, but what was my next move going to be? I stared at the screen and eventually began to type. I would have to play along to get any answers, 'If you are an older form of myself you would know that I do not believe in anything supernatural. Repeat the exercise tonight, but I am not going to write my diary entry until after I have seen your email. Your words should tell me exactly what I have done.'

I wandered downstairs and washed up my cup and plate. Then I opened the mail which consisted of an electricity bill and an envelope inviting me to purchase 'superfast broadband.' Both seemed like forms of extortion in an era where it is nigh on impossible to live without the Internet. Before long I'd bounded back up the stairs to find another email awaiting my attention. Without hesitation I clicked it open and perused its contents.

'This website has strict procedures and it will not allow the passing of information relating to events that haven't occurred yet to the younger version of the two participants. All such communications are blocked. I do not understand the reason for this, but being a scientific man I am sure you can conceive that future forms of technology will seem supernatural to you. I can only repeat the exercise with today's entry but if you try to read it before writing the diary entry the email will be blank due to content-blocking. This is why I said to wait until the next day to open the email.'

If this was a game of chess it seemed like checkmate, but if the mystery emailer really was an older version of myself, maybe I should have thought of him as being on the same side as me. In which case, who would be the real opponent?

No, I still viewed him (or her – let's not be sexist again) as an impostor that needed to be outsmarted. But just then the irony struck me. I'd spent my whole life feeling like I was faking it, but now *I* was the real person and somebody else was pretending to be Steven Jones! 'If there is a god he's got a sense of humour,' I thought to myself.

No, let's leave God out of it. Tempting though it was to pray for release from this maze of confusion, I had to keep my thoughts strictly scientific to stay sane.

I remembered snatches of the previous night's dream and suddenly it made sense. I wanted to glue the pieces of my life back together but I was lost in a labyrinth. And if I really had embarked on some kind of psychological chase like 'The Da Vinci Code,' just what was the Holy Grail that I was searching for?

I remembered the blank photograph in the passport in my dream and it became obvious.

Of course – myself!

Chapter 11

It was Monday lunchtime, and as the three ladies walked from the counter to their usual table in the Hummingbird Coffee Shop, Anne's cup was rattling noisily in its saucer.

'You seem a bit shaky today,' observed Catherine as they took their seats and two of them flung off their outer garments in a flurry of activity.

'Oh gosh, is it that obvious?' Anne exclaimed, without even taking her dark fake-leather jacket off, 'What a weekend! The truth is I think Steven is having a breakdown of some kind.'

Her two friends looked at her in silent inquisitiveness.

'He completely lost it the other morning. He thinks somebody is drugging him.'

'I thought he was drugging himself?' enquired Catherine in her usual direct manner.

'So did I, but he was absolutely crazed on Saturday and he emptied the coffee tin into the rubbish bin, saying that there were white crystals in it and that somebody was trying to send him mad.'

'Who would do that?' said Jane.

'He thinks Martin is pushing hard drugs on him, spiking his drinks and even mixing it in with the coffee at home, but the thing is, Martin never comes to the house, they always meet at that toffs' pub, the Black Dog.'

'Oh, I quite like it there,' defended Catherine, 'Lovely Food. Matt and I go there sometimes. I've never seen your husband there though.' She paused, 'So do you think he should see someone, like a psychiatrist? I mean, I think all men should – I can't understand them anyway, but it sounds like he's gone one step beyond.'

'Maybe,' replied Anne, thoughtfully staring into her teacup, 'He can't carry on like this. I asked him why he thinks he's been spiked and he started rambling on about hallucinating and seeing mysterious emails. He was pulling the kitchen to pieces, opening cupboards and staring in tins. He tipped the sugar bowl into the bin too. He said "What better place to hide white crystals than in a bowl of white crystals?" He's not well, I'm sure of it.'

'So what can you do?' asked Jane, the youngest of the three women, sweeping back her long auburn hair as she spoke.

'God knows! He'd go nuts if he thought I was arranging something behind his back. We did speak about it, well, shout about it. He says he doesn't need any therapy, he just needs people to stop interfering. And here's another thing – he cooked himself some bacon and you should have seen him lifting it up and examining it, as though even that was contaminated. It's paranoia; there's only me in the house and why would I try to get him to go off his trolley? I think he's crazy enough without me spiking his food!'

'I don't want to be nosey, but you and Steven don't do a lot together, do you?' posed Catherine delicately, before burying her nose into a a cup of frothy cappuccino.

'We just don't get time really. He works funny shifts at the pub, and me, well, you know how busy we are at Jessop's sweat-shop.'

'I just think...' Catherine thought carefully, 'I just think that perhaps a bit of distraction would do him good – would do both of you good. Something fun. Heavens, even a bit of romance, why not?'

'You've got to be joking!' defended Anne, 'We're not teenagers. We've got bills to pay.'

Jane mimed stifling a yawn before piping up. 'But life shouldn't be just about paying bills to exist. Life is ride – a roller-coaster as the song says. You can't just exist like a gherkin in a pickle jar.'

'You're right,' said Anne, 'But that's how we're all living now with this *cost of living* crisis, just working to survive. All that technology they foisted on us has done naff all to give us more leisure time. Remember how they said that machines would be doing all the work for us in the future. Huh, total pipe dream. The machines do the work and the fat cats scoop up all the money and sack the workers.'

'Hark at you, you little socialist!' laughed Catherine, 'You'll be back to counting the beans for them in half an hour.' Just then the ladies were interrupted by the usual tall young man strategically sliding a tray containing three baguettes in between them. He didn't want to interrupt the debate today.

Anne responded in a hushed tone, 'That's what I mean – we *are* the pickles in the jars, and the jars sit on the shelves of the wealthy. They make the rules and restrict the money supply, trapping us so that we can only do things their way.'

'So, hang about,' ventured Jane, 'Maybe the free ones in society are people like Steven and Martin. They're trying to break out of the jar whatever way they can.'

'No, that's silly!' countered Anne, 'You don't find freedom by frying your own brain.' And with that she chomped down heavily on her Brie and grape baguette.

'Do you not?' asked Catherine rhetorically, 'Look at that tea you're drinking. Why do you drink that?'

'Tea revives you,' spluttered Anne, recalling an old saying her grandmother used to often repeat.

'Right. And that's making your little chink in the glass of the jar for today. We're all doing it in our own way – trying to find freedom. Tea, coffee, fags, drink, you name it...'

'It's a cup of bleeding tea!' laughed Anne.

Catherine elaborated further, 'What I'm saying is that the pair of you got married to go through life together, but you're like two lost souls again now. Steven is doing his thing and you're doing yours. His thing might be sending him nuts but at least he's trying to find freedom.'

'Since when did you become the agony aunt?' mocked Anne, 'Look I'll think about it, but I can't see the romance coming back. Once you've squeezed all the toothpaste out of the tube you'll never get it back in again. I think that's how it works with all that romantic stuff. We're done and dusted on all that malarkey.'

'If it's that bad I'm staying single,' joked Jane, and while breaking her *full English breakfast* baguette in half she added, 'And that means I can eat as many of these as I want and not give a damn about my figure!'

The three women laughed together. Maybe Jane was the closest to finding freedom after all.

Chapter 12 (Steven)

Alright, I'll admit it, I did throw the coffee and the sugar in the bin, but you'd do the same if this happened to you. I seriously *did* wonder what was going on and I could only conclude that somebody was trying to pack me off to the funny farm. I didn't trust Martin after he spiked my drink that time and Anne's behaviour was something of a mystery too, so I could only trust myself. I'll tell you what happened on Saturday and maybe you'll see my point of view.

When I'd gone to bed the night before I didn't write anything in my diary at all, as I'd decided to leave it until the morning. Yes, I ignored the instructions from the mystery emailer. The email from my supposed future self was there in my inbox waiting to be opened, so I got up on Saturday morning and waited for Anne to go off on her weekly shopping jaunt around the town. I went into the study, turned on the computer and opened the email, and you know what, it was blank, just as he said it would be if I tried to view it before writing the diary entry.

It seemed to me that whatever joker had come up with this whole ruse had concocted some lame excuse about the website not passing on information about the future. I don't know how he was doing this but it just seemed like a trick to me. Come on out, Derren Brown, I've rumbled you!

So I got my little black book from the bedroom drawer and returned to the study. I was going to write my diary entry, right there in front of the computer. Well, what happened was so bizarre that I had to conclude that I was hallucinating.

As I began to write in the book the very same words began to appear on the screen. Initially I just wrote the date of the day before – Friday March 18th – well, he could have guessed that bit I'm sure, but how was it possible that the following words appeared in an open email at exactly the moment that I scrawled them in my diary, literally letter by letter?

'Got up and made tea and toast. Went to the study to open the email and it appeared to contain today's diary entry. No idea how the sender is doing this so I challenged him to send today's entry and planned to open it before I'd written anything in this diary...'

The weird thing was, it became hard to concentrate on writing a diary entry for the day before when something this surreal was going on right in front of me on the screen, so I doubted my own sanity. It was then that I remembered seeing those white granules in the coffee tin. I rushed downstairs into the kitchen and I grabbed the receptacle, opening it and peering inside. The evidence was there – small white crystals reflecting the kitchen light back at me as I gazed into the brown depths. It had to go. I rushed over to the pedal bin and shot the whole lot in.

It was at this moment that the back door opened and in walked Anne with two heavy bags of groceries.

'Oh hi,' she said, 'That traffic was murder getting into the town centre today. They're digging up the roads again...' It was then that she glanced down at the coffee granules that had missed the bin. 'What in God's name are you doing?'

'That's what I was going to ask you,' I replied, 'This coffee is contaminated. From now on I am preparing all my own food and drinks. Someone is interfering with my mind and I'm going to get to the bottom of it.'

'You what?' asked Anne incredulously as she deposited the shopping bags onto the work surface.

'I don't know who it is. I don't trust Martin any more. He's already spiked my drink once, but I'm still seeing things that aren't there. It's a conspiracy, I tell you!' My eyes fixed on the sugar bowl. I leaned over and grabbed it from the shelf, taking off the lid and holding it out to Anne, 'What do you see?'

'Sugar,' came the feeble reply.

'But is it just sugar? How can you tell? If I wanted to get somebody to take some white granules what better place could there be to hide them than in with the sugar?'

'Why would anybody want you to take white granules?'

'Come on Anne, you know Martin dabbles with drugs. He wants to get me hooked. I expect he gets a cut of the profits from that dodgy dealer he meets.'

'What *are* you talking about?'

'Look. *You* don't drink coffee and you don't take sugar, so if he hides the granules only in things that *I* consume, he's covered his back.'

'That makes no sense. If he really wants to get people hooked on drugs why not get us both addicted to the stuff and double his cut of the profits?'

Anne had raised a valid point but I wasn't going to concede. She hadn't seen those words appearing on the computer screen like that, so she couldn't really judge what had happened. 'What if it's not even Martin?' I ventured.

'What are you saying? Nobody has been in here apart from us two. None of this makes any sense.'

'Exactly!' I replied 'Are you working with him or for him?'

I said this in a jokey tone hoping to raise a serious point without causing offence, but Anne looked wounded. 'For crying out loud. I've never even met the bloke. And I'm too busy to get involved in his, er, activities. I've got spreadsheets coming out of my ears at the moment. Why would I want a husband who's losing the plot? Come on Steven, this is ridiculous!'

It was as though the use of the word 'ridiculous' spurred me into action and I clumsily shot the contents of the sugar bowl into the bin.

Anne just stared in disbelief but I was already pulling open cupboards. I scratched my head trying to remember all the foods that I ate that Anne never touched. I gazed at the various jars of spices and sauces, but nothing really leapt out at me as something that only the male half of the household was likely to consume. In truth I didn't know what I was doing but I pulled out a pot of jam, unscrewed the lid and sniffed it. There was a large tin of cocoa powder in the cupboard too, so I ripped off the plastic top and stared into it, giving the impression that I knew what I was looking for, but in truth, apart from sweet coffee our diet was pretty similar, so I was just clutching at straws.

I closed the cupboard. The red mist was beginning to clear but I was still lost in a maze of confusion. I took a deep breath, 'Look, I think I've been experiencing hallucinations. I don't know what is causing them but I need to eliminate the options. Just bear with me. I'm going to get to the bottom of this.'

I had levelled with Anne, but as she looked at the flurry of brown and white granules that had missed the bin it only added up to one thing in her mind – madness. 'You need to get help,' she asserted, 'Some therapy - just look at the state of this kitchen. This is insanity.'

'No,' I said, 'Seeing words appear one by one on a computer screen as you write them down in front of it – that's insanity!'

'What are you talking about?'

'This is the kind of stuff that I'm trying to get my head around. Something is going on. It's like some sort of elaborate trick, but the trick is just going on and on and it isn't amusing at all.'

'Look, just take a break,' Anne remonstrated, 'Shut the computer down. Go and have a beer, whatever it takes. I'll put these groceries away and we'll talk about it.'

She disappeared into the downstairs loo, so I retrieved a dustpan and brush from the broom cupboard and cleared up the mess. If only the mental confusion was as easy to clear up as a few coffee granules, but I suppose I'd have to wait for whatever was in that coffee or sugar to wear off before I could think straight. I grabbed a bottle of Oakbourne Brewery's 'Quince Orchard Ale' from the fridge and went back up to the study. I pulled out the drawer from under the desk where I keep a handy bottle opener and yanked off the lid. Maybe she was right that I needed a break, but I just couldn't push the whole affair out of my mind like that. I took a hefty swig from the bottle and savoured the hoppy bite of the ale. Then I picked up that familiar pencil and began anxiously tapping it rhythmically on the desk, as though trying to drum up some kind of plan of action.

The email was still open with the words from my diary larger than life on the screen. I savoured the bubbles on my tongue before swallowing the beer. Had I typed those words myself without remembering it? Maybe I had multiple personality disorder, believing that things I'd typed myself were being sent anonymously. Maybe I was becoming schizophrenic, unsure of what was real and what was not.

I eventually deduced that I had to carry on as normal, so I closed the email and continued writing the diary entry for the day before. Apart from the mystery email there wasn't really much to report. It had been just another routine day at work with the usual friendly but ultimately meaningless chat from Anabelle, a couple of conversations about the new ales we were going to have at the Unicorn and dealing with a group of lads that were getting a bit out of hand and had to be asked to calm down.

I then started thinking about Schrödinger's Cat, as we all do from time to time, right? Bear with me, but this is a theory relating to quantum particles in physics. It has been established that until a particle is actually observed it can be in any number of positions and states simultaneously. It all sounds a bit wacky, but when you look at life in detail it does all get a bit bonkers.

In Schrödinger's thought experiment there is a cat in a box and whether or not a fatal substance is released depends entirely on whether or not a particle decays and this is a 50/50 chance. The point is that if there is nobody to open the box and observe things, the cat must be both alive and dead at the same time, as the particle that determines this can be in both states until it is observed.

Now, sometimes I think it is better to keep things this way in life generally, and the mystery email is a case in point. Curiosity would have me go straight back on the computer and open it again. My head felt clear now, so if somebody really had spiked my coffee and I had hallucinated the whole thing, there would be no more words in the message than when I closed it down, but if it really was some kind of communication from a future 'me,' then the entire diary entry that I'd just penned would now be in the email when I opened it. So you see, until I open that email, both versions of reality are possible. And keeping things that way gives us the illusion that we have some kind of control over our lives. Not choosing to observe means allowing ourselves more possibilities. Or so it seems.

So I decided to remain in control for as long as I could. I closed the computer down and moved my chair over to the window. I finished my bottle of beer while watching the magnolia tree sway in the breeze outside. There were a few pink petals on it now and it was nice just to sit and watch the world outside. And as I observed I wondered if I would actually open the email again at all. It was bliss not knowing, and this sounds weird, doesn't it? Especially when I said that my whole problem in life was *never knowing*. And for the first time in many years I'd forgotten about *impostor syndrome* and *dissociation* and acting and the Hallway to Hell and faking it to make it and all those things that made me feel like a pickle in a jar on somebody's shelf.

Just for a moment, I felt free.

Chapter 13 (Steven)

Curiosity is a funny thing. It's like a nagging child, and until you give it the attention it demands the nagging gets louder and louder.

I'd enjoyed my moment of peace by the window in the study but I couldn't sit there all day. Life had to carry on and I went downstairs to think about a late breakfast. Or was it an early lunch? Either way, a bacon sandwich fitted the bill perfectly. The thing was, Anne was sitting at the table in the kitchen doing a crossword, but I didn't want to offend her by examining the food as closely as I wanted to.

I found it hard to imagine that she would be behind all this but I had to protect my own mind from further chemical intrusions. I lifted each rasher out of the packet with the tongs and held it up, taking a good look at it before dunking it onto the grill pan. As with the jam and the cocoa, I really didn't know what I was looking for. Who's ever heard of bacon dipped in cocaine or injected with LSD? That would be insane, wouldn't it?

She glanced over and I could tell that she didn't approve of the way I was holding up the strips of pig meat. She felt as though it was her that I was holding up and examining. She returned to her crossword. A few minutes later she did me a favour and took her cup of tea and her newspaper through to the lounge.

Bear with me, but bacon is a bit like our marriage really. The scent, i.e. the promise of it, actually seems better than the thing itself. Living with Anne seemed so appealing at the start, like an answer to all life's problems. I felt that we were a team, and two of you facing the world and all its madness has got to be better than one. But a few years down the line it's as though life couldn't keep up its own act and I've reverted to playing a solo role in a play where I don't even understand the script.

The bacon crispened up, giving off that tantalising scent, and before long I was biting into that perfect blend of textures – soft bread, crispy bacon and a dollop of ketchup. This was going to be a good day.

I had decided to challenge the real impostor head on. Once the sandwich was finished I would delete the last email, effectively deleting my own insecurity in the process. Then I would ask him or her a direct question.

Before long I was back upstairs with the computer turned on. I hovered the cursor over the envelope logo. One click would give the option to either erase the email or open it. The temptation to look and see if the diary entry I'd written just minutes ago had been replicated was immense, but no, I was going to take control. Within an instant the mystery message had been expunged. Shrödinger's email was no more. Or should I say 'Schrödinger's chat?'

I then typed in that familiar seven-digit number to bring up the original red web page, which now came up as a suggestion after I'd tapped in just the first few digits. The vivid screen appeared and in the familiar text box I entered my question:

'Is there something that you want to tell me?'

This time there would be no pacing around the room, no nervous tapping of pencils on teeth or keyboard, I just sat, staring at the screen as though I was staring out an adversary in a game of chess. I was calm. Waiting, waiting, waiting.

Take all day to respond if you like. I'm playing this game *my* way now.

Chapter 14

The young man behind the counter at the Hummingbird Coffee Shop is called Jacob. He is 24 years old and he has always been interested in art. He painted the pictures of various flowers that adorn the walls of the establishment. It is his auntie who owns the café and she is the sister of his mother who is sadly no longer alive. She lost her battle with cancer at 46.

Jacob lives with his father in a village called Little Buckby which is about four miles from Wickersby town centre on the flat side of town. The A48 is dead straight all the way into Wickersby on this side because it follows the route of an old Roman road, although it deviates from the straight line to bypass both Little Buckby and Great Buckby which is another mile or so along the Roman road.

Jacob's father owns a garage in Little Buckby and he has thrown himself into his work since losing his wife. He always wanted Jacob to follow in his footsteps and work with cars in some way but Jacob was always interested in art. He had a fascination with impressionist paintings from his early teenage years and tried in vain to replicate the style. He went to uni to study art and when he was back at home in the holidays he worked at the coffee shop to help to fund his course.

Sadly, the degree hasn't helped him since he completed it a year ago and serving drinks and snacks at the Hummingbird is now his full-time job. His auntie was particularly proud of the way he completed his degree in spite of losing his mother halfway through his studies. It wasn't easy to concentrate while having to deal with grief at such a young age but somehow he managed it. If only society would recognise his efforts and reward him with a career in his chosen field, but it often doesn't work like that, does it? Sometimes he wonders if his dad was right all along. There's always plenty of work if you learn a trade but then he was never interested in grease and pistons.

Jacob quite enjoys people-watching however, and the Hummingbird is a great place for this when it's not too busy. He has noticed the three women who often come in from the accountancy office at lunhctimes and of the three he thinks Jane is the nicest. She's only a few years older than him and she is definitely the most open-minded of the three. He isn't so keen on Catherine and Anne seems like the glue that holds the threesome together, ever practical and diplomatic.

And does he have a girlfriend? Er, well no. His father has a few homophobic tendencies and wondered if his son was gay.

'Would it matter if I was?' Jacob used to reply. He had several gay friends at uni and they all got on like a house on fire, but in truth Jacob is just a bit on the shy side. All the way through uni the other lads got the girls and he just buried his head in books on Monet and Renoir. And now that his studying days are over he wonders how on earth he is going to meet someone. Most people seem to use the Internet to set up dates these days but it all seems so artificial.

'So you're my date. Am I supposed to fall madly in love now, or should it take a few meetings?'

No, that way never appealed to Jacob at all. He just hopes that one day somebody nice will walk into the coffee shop and get chatting to him.

And does he like living with his father?

Well, it's OK I suppose. He saves a fortune on rent that way and on coffee shop wages he couldn't afford to rent on his own anyway. He'd need to meet that mythical partner just to help keep a roof over his head. His father watches 'Formula 1' and a lot of programmes like 'Top Gear' which aren't Jacob's cup of tea at all, so Jacob spends a lot of his time in his room. It's not ideal but it'll have to do for now.

He quite enjoys his job so the fact that it was Monday didn't really bother him at all. The three ladies were in as usual and were now polishing off their baguettes. One of them had been going on about her husband having some kind of nervous breakdown, or so it seemed. It was quiet enough to listen in that lunchtime.

'You know what, I'm going to have a chocolate eclair. To hell with the expense,' declared Jane.

'You're pushing the boat out,' was Catherine's response 'A *full English breakfast* baguette *and* a chocolate eclair!'

'Yeah, why not?'

'You know that means we'll all have to have one?' said Anne. Catherine winced. How was she ever going to lose weight with these two around. 'Go on then,' she chipped in reluctantly, 'You might as well order three.'

Jane fist-pumped the air, as though declaring a victory over stuffiness and routine and she wandered up to the counter to speak to the young man. It was odd really. The times that they had been there for lunch and none of them knew his name or anything about him.

Before long Jane was seated back at the table and the young man wandered over with a plate and three eclairs.

'Looks delicious,' remarked Jane as he placed them down.

'Enjoy!' announced the young man.

While Jane took a bite, sending a dollop of cream cascading onto her plate, Anne launched into the next topic for the ladies to deliberate upon, which was really just a different aspect of the same topic.

'I've been thinking a lot about what I read in Steven's diaries. The clue to understanding what is going on with him must surely be there.'

'Have you been snooping again?' chipped in Catherine.

'Well, after the bacon inspection I offered to talk about it but he just disappeared back up to the study for most of the day. On Sunday he said he was going for a long walk to clear his head, and as he'd given me no sensible explanation for his behaviour I just had to find out for myself.'

'And what did you find out?'

'Well, he seems to think of his life as though he is an actor playing a part, maybe playing lots of parts, and this made me think about life in general.'

'Sounds a bit Shakespearean,' quipped Jane while swallowing down another mouthful of chocolate eclair. She gulped, 'The world's a stage and each must play a part...'

'That was Elvis, Jane,' joked Catherine, but Anne continued before she had a chance to sing 'Are You Lonesome Tonight?' in a deep *Elvis* voice. She knew Catherine wasn't keen on the heavier subjects and always tried to find ways to lighten the tone.

'I mean, he could be right, you know? Maybe we are all actors really.'

'Now hang on,' mused Jane, 'If we are all actors there can be no right or wrong, as we are all just playing a role and have no choice about what that role is. And that means terrorists and paedophiles have no choice either.'

'Well, it's just a theory,' Anne conceded, 'But maybe those kind of people are just ill. Maybe if they could come forward and get help before the twisted thoughts take control we could save a lot of people from having their lives messed up.'

'Jesus, you two!' exclaimed Catherine, 'Give me a break.'

Jane ignored the interjection, 'So if they're ill what treatment would you propose?'

'I don't know. How about if they could just come forward anonymously and get some kind of drug that suppresses whatever is going on in their heads?

'You mean the same way that a depressive person or somebody with anxiety issues can?' asked Jane. 'Hmm, well I guess if it stops the victims from suffering...'

Catherine broke the thoughtful silence, 'Those guys are just sick in the head and should be lobotomised!'

'Thanks for your insight,' joked Anne sarcastically.

Noticing that Catherine was clearly uncomfortable with this particular topic, or any heavy subject matter, Jane changed the tone, 'Well, that's another edition of Anne and Jane's philosophy hour over. We'll be back the same time tomorrow.'

Catherine smiled, 'I just prefer not to think about things like that. I know that such people exist and that we have to do something about it, but are they ill or are they just psychopaths? I don't know.'

'Psychopathy is an illness,' Anne chipped in.

'Smart arse!' grinned Catherine, 'Anyway, what's any of this got to do with Steven and his complexities?'

'I dunno really,' mumbled Anne, 'It just made me think a bit. If he feels like he's acting the role of Steven Jones, maybe we're all acting a role, and once you realise that, you have to accept that it includes everyone, even criminals.'

Catherine looked up from her cup; 'And tyrants like Hitler and Stalin?'

'The whole bleeding lot,' said Anne.

'No, I'm not comfortable with that. They're just men. They're different to us.'

'Ah, the old anti-men thing again!' grinned Jane, 'How does Matt put up with it?'

'He's different,' said Catherine, 'I know him.'

Anne decided to keep pressing; 'Do you really know anyone?'

'Here we go again,' sighed Catherine.

'I mean I'm lying next to Steven at night and his head is just inches away, but what goes on inside it might as well be what goes on on Mars. Unless you can actually be inside someone else's mind and think their thoughts you can't really say that you know them at all.'

'But you're trying to understand, right?'

'Precisely,' stated Anne.

Jane backtracked, 'There are women criminals too. I don't think that's fair to say they're all men, Catherine.'

'Huh,' came the response, 'It's the blokes that drive the women to it!'

The pair knew she was joking and decided to let it go.

'I find it weird,' Jane directed at Catherine, 'There you are slagging men off all the time, yet you've got a loyal boyfriend, and here I am saying they're no different to us and I'm on my own.'

'You've plenty of time,' comforted Catherine, 'You're still young.'

Just then there was a clatter as the door to the café burst open. It was a white-painted wooden door with two columns of glass squares from the top to the bottom. It banged against the wall with the force as a man stumbled in looking decidedly worse for wear.

'See what I mean,' mumbled Catherine, rolling her eyes, 'Look at the state they let themselves get into!'

'He's just playing a part,' quipped Jane wittily.

'Look at the facts, it's half past one and he looks like he's just dragged himself out of his pit,' whispered Catherine. Anne and Jane decided not to add fuel to the fire and sat silently sipping their hot drinks.

The man was soon seated with a tall glass of iced coffee.

'That'll be great for a hangover I reckon,' remarked the ever-forthright Catherine, but adopting a gentler stance she added, 'I wonder why people get into such a state.'

'Like I said, unless you can actually get into their heads you'll never know,' said Anne, 'I just hope Steven isn't going the same way as this poor soul. I don't know what's going on with him but I really couldn't put up with him getting into a mess like that. It was bad enough him doing that *bull in a china shop* impression in the kitchen the other day!'

'Ah, there *is* a limit to your patience then?' mused Catherine.

'Yeah, I suppose there is,' Anne conceded.

A lot of rustling seemed to be emanating from the dishevelled man's table. There followed sniffs and sighs as he slurped from the delicate-looking glass.

'I think he's in trouble,' Jane sympathised quietly.

The other two looked blank, so she elaborated, 'I mean, I think he's got a problem. He's clearly on a downward spiral.'

'Well done, Sherlock,' returned the acid-wit of Catherine, 'Tell us something we can't see for ourselves.'

The man reached into his pocket and pulled out an envelope which looked a bit crumpled and had clearly been opened before. Straightening out the piece of paper that was inside it on the table to read it, he knocked the envelope onto the floor as a breeze from the open door sent it in the direction of the table of the three ladies, landing against Anne's foot.

She gazed down below the tablecloth, as though she was assessing it before deciding to make a grab for it. As she picked up the brown envelope she noticed a name written on the outside in bold letters, Martin Wilson.

'Oh my God!' she thought to herself, 'I know that name. He's Steven's friend, Martin!' She decided to keep this knowledge under her hat, at least for the time being.

Chapter 15 (Steven)

The reply didn't come for nearly two days. My future self must be a lazy so-and-so. I expect he doesn't even look at his emails at weekends. He probably spends his Saturdays sampling real ales and his Sundays writing tasting notes in his little black books.

Well, I spent my Sunday on a long walk. I thought it would do me good to get some endorphins flowing around my system and I began by wandering down to Millbrook Stores in the square at the end of our road. I carried on into the town centre, passing the Black Dog, the Hummingbird Coffee Shop and the Unicorn, wandering into the churchyard of All Saints, which is the central church in Wickersby, a large stone place of worship with an imposing square tower. Well, who should I bump into but that vicar I told you about, you know the one who said he'd let me have whatever I wanted etched upon my gravestone that time I met him before? He was dressed in a white robe and was leaving the church after a service.

Now, I've always called him the Reverend Reuben but Reuben is his Christian name. I'm not even sure of his surname. He still recognised me from our casual conversation before, in fact he greeted me with the phrase 'never knowing' to prove that he still remembered it.

Now, the Reverend Reuben is an Afro-Caribbean man and I'll be honest, you don't come across a lot of diversity in Wickersby. He told me a bit about his life, growing up in London and then moving out here as his second parish. He was uncertain as to how the locals would take to him but he'd found everyone very welcoming. But why Wickersby?

Well, he told me a story about the little church on the hill where I got married – Saint Cecilia's. Apparently many centuries ago an ancient priest found himself lost up on the moors in the mist. He prayed that he would find his way back to civilisation, and when the mist cleared he found himself at a vantage-point overlooking the town. He fell to his knees and gave thanks, promising to build a church on that spot to show his gratitude to the Almighty.

Now, as you know I don't really go in for this kind of stuff but the Reverend Reuben had found the story fascinating and interpreted this as a sign that this was the parish for him. He explained that he had felt somewhat lost in the mist himself at the time. He had just had his first child and he had decided that somewhere quieter and more rural than South London would be more suitable for raising a family. His wife, who had many friends in London, was quite reluctant but, filled with the joy of a child, she decided to capitulate and give Wickersby a try.

He then informed me that although All Saints was the main church, there were three others around the town that he was responsible for, as well as that lovely little church up on the hill. I hadn't been quite sure where to walk but the power of suggestion is strong and this tale seemed to turn my aimless amble into a mission with a destination. I was going to go up on the moors.

Concluding his potted life story he turned to me and said, 'Sometimes answers come in unexpected ways. You've still got a lot of your time ahead of you I'm sure. You may feel that *never knowing* sums up your life now, but who knows how you'll feel when you're my age?'

This puzzled me, for I had assumed that the Reverend Reuben was a similar age to me but he was clearly significantly older. He continued, 'I've noted your request for future incumbents of this parish should I move on or pop my clogs. It's not for me to come between a man and his last request. There is only one judge of all of us after all, and if you change your mind about this request you've plenty of years to update the records.'

I smiled, 'I appreciate that. And thanks for noting it down.'

'Well, my doors are always open if you fancy a chat. Perhaps we all feel a bit like that ancient priest at times.'

'You're not wrong,' I agreed, 'Lost in the mist, right?'

'You got it!' laughed the friendly vicar, and with a swish of his robe he turned and walked off down the gently curving path through the gravestones.

I continued out of the other side of the churchyard and through the suburban streets towards the hillside, which looms up from the end of every road in this part of town, but I didn't make it to Saint Cecilia's. I just changed my mind. You're allowed to do that, even the vicar said so.

It seemed as though the further I got from home, the further I was from receiving that all-important reply to my question. The wacky website had got me hooked. It felt almost wrong to go trekking up a large hillside to a church which was at least an hour's walk from my home, so what did I do? I walked around the edge of Wickersby in a huge circle, which meant that my wander would take me a good few hours but if I got the sudden urge to check my email account I could be home within half an hour from anywhere on the route. Strangely the nagging sensation dissipated and I was out so long that Anne thought I'd injured myself. Or that I'd been mugged.

'Actually I've been chatting to a vicar!' I informed her.

'So what was the reply to the email?' you are wondering.

Well it was Monday morning when the following nugget of information dropped into my inbox.

'Greetings. You asked for some advice and I am unsure how you might take this. I am an old man and I can't remember how I used to react to weird ideas, but over the course of this century scientists have begun to investigate the claims of the world's religions thoroughly and without prejudice. No conclusion has been made regarding the existence of God but it has been proven beyond reasonable doubt that reverse-praying is more effective than straightforward praying. By this I mean that praying for the very opposite to your desired outcome yields the best results. This is an accepted statistical fact in my time. I'm trying to help you, which means that I'm trying to help myself, so please pray for my / your premature death.'

I sat dumbfounded. This was the most ridiculous email I had ever set my eyes upon, and how did this piece of information get past the electronic censors? I thought the emails couldn't contain anything about the future. The trouble was, the sender had got me hooked again. Was this the intention all along?

I walked back and forth across that patterned rug scratching my head. Remember what I said about curiosity nagging until it gets what it wants? It seemed that it hadn't had its fill yet and now there was just another layer in the 'Da Vinci Code' style psychological puzzle for me to decode – first the hallucination, then the mystery emailer and now an unwanted dose of religion with an added twist.

Being Monday, it was my day off work and Anne was at work herself. I was glad of this. I wasn't sure how I would have got through the day with this latest conundrum occupying my every thought. I needed to talk to somebody, but not a therapist like Anne suggested, it needed to be somebody who has experienced this kind of derangement first hand. And who was the one person that sprang to mind?

Yes, you've guessed it – the one person that got me into this labyrinthine mess in the first place. The one and only Martin Wilson!

Chapter 16 (Steven)

I rang Martin and he agreed to meet me at the Black Dog at 1pm. You could call it a liquid lunch I guess.

It is a short walk from my home to this pub and I felt positive, determined to wrestle with things until Martin and I had unpicked the web of thoughts that surrounded me. Martin had experienced all kinds of mind-bending realities, thanks to his relentless dabbling with pills and powders, so maybe he was just the man to apply some lateral thinking to my conundrum. Or so I hoped.

I was there first so I texted him to say that I was getting the first round in. I grimaced as I spotted the 'Cherry Tree Ale' pump, recalling my experience of the beer with a mystery active ingredient that had opened up this whole can of worms.

'Hi,' said the curly-haired denim-clad barmaid, who looked about thirty, 'What can I get you?'

'A pint of Guinness please,' I ordered cautiously. I knew exactly how the black stuff should taste so I'd know for sure if my drink had been interfered with. 'And a pint of your house lager please,' I added, pre-empting Martin's unimaginative selection.

Having paid and waited for the Guinness to settle, I picked up the two glasses and took my place on a stool at a high round table near a painting of a fox hunt. 'Blood-thirsty toffs!' I thought to myself. Having taken a few sips, I wiped away the froth moustache and began to run over everything in my mind. I needed to present the facts coherently to Martin. Like a computer, if you program rubbish into people you get rubbish out. No, I had to present the events clearly, concisely, and most importantly, in a believable way – now *there's* a challenge!

I didn't have long to prepare before Martin walked through the door in his familiar black bomber jacket. Nobody had told him that this fashion died out in the 1990s, not that I gave a monkey's for fashion anyway.

'Hey!' he greeted me. I raised my glass as a friendly gesture. 'Good man,' he declared picking up the pint of pale-looking lager before even sitting down, 'Glad you didn't get me any of that old ditchwater stuff you drink. What's with the Guinness? No real ales you like?'

'No,' I said flatly, 'Not really.'

'What's up with you? You sound serious as cancer!'

'Rhythm is a dancer!' I replied, spotting his reference to an old nineties hit, 'It's not just your fashion sense that's stuck in the past.'

'Oi, oi, lay off!' joked Martin, 'Anyway, why the long face?'

'There's been a lot going on,' I began, 'And I need your thoughts on it all.'

'Yeah, why not, forget the small talk and cut straight to the chase,' grinned Martin sarcastically. 'Hey, she's a bit tasty,' he added, clocking the curly-haired barmaid before seizing his pint and taking a hefty lug.

Ignoring his levity, I handed Martin a brown envelope with his name on. I'm not sure why I wrote his full name on it. I think it was in case he forgot his name in a drug-addled stupor.

'Inside this is a slip of paper with a web address on it. Now, I discovered this by punching in that number that appeared in the hallucinations we had when we were tripping out on that weird powder you got.'

Martin took the envelope, 'And you want me to take a look?'

'Right. There's just a red screen, a box for your email address and a box for a question. You can ask anything you want but I've written the question that I would like you to ask on the slip of paper too.'

'Blimey, you're well prepared. So what's the question?'

'You just ask "Is there something you want to tell me?" Now, when you get the reply it will look like it comes from your own email address. Don't be alarmed. You can ask whatever you like of it after that, but I'd like you to save the reply to this particular question and forward it to me. It's a mystery that I need to solve.'

It was Martin's turn to talk, so I took a hefty swig from my pint glass.

'OK, I'll do it, but this isn't a one-way street. I want to know what happened to you now.'

I collected my nerves as I placed my glass back onto the beer mat.

'This is going to sound insane, but the person replying to me via that site says that he is an older version of myself and he gave me the weirdest piece of advice, telling me to pray for the opposite of anything I want to happen.' Martin's face was starting to look confused so I slammed in the punchline as though making a *hit and run*, 'And ultimately he wants me to pray for my own death.'

'What the...?' began Martin, 'I'd say the bloke's a loony.'

'But he's a clever loony.' I continued, 'You see he is also giving me information that he couldn't possibly know.'

'What, like having a spot on your bum or something?' came the typically ribald reply.

I laughed before regaining my composure, 'No, it's more personal than that. He seems to be able to quote passages from my own diaries. Not even Anne knows what I write in them.'

'Hang on,' spluttered Martin, 'Surely all you have to do is tell him to quote an entry you haven't written yet. That'll screw him up.'

'Tried it. He says he can't pass on any info about my own future as the system will block it and obviously if the diary entry hasn't been written it's still in the future.'

'He can't pass it on because he hasn't got it!' laughed Martin, 'It's a con. Total B.S.'

Just then the barmaid came over to collect some glasses from the empty table next to us. Martin smiled at her, 'You alright?'

'Not bad,' she said, 'How's your beer?'

'Top notch,' he replied and then repeated this, with added confidence. Was he referring to the beer or the lady who served it? As she walked away his attention returned to me.

'OK, humour me,' I continued, 'Let's just say that the way in which this all happened made his claim seem plausible. Why would a future version of me want me to pray for my own death?'

Martin sounded excitable, 'Look, I think it's absolute drivel, mate, but I suppose if a future version of you believed in this *opposite praying* thing maybe he has got something terminal like cancer and he thinks if he gets you to pray for the opposite for many years it won't kill him.'

'Good,' I say, having thought of that scenario myself, 'But now let's flip it. Say he's made up all the flannel about science proving that reverse-praying works to trick me. What would be his motive then?'

'Well, I suppose he might actually want to die before the disease gets bad so that he doesn't have to suffer with it. This is assuming he believes that praying works in the normal kind of way. But it's still cobblers because you don't believe in any sort of praying so why would he, if he is you?'

'People change I guess,' I concede, 'A lot of people turn to religion when faced with death. So whether he believes in reverse-praying or in straightforward praying, you think that a future version of me would have my best interest, which is his own best interest, in mind.'

'Yeah, but it's not a future version of you. It's a nutter!'

'OK, OK. Now, think about the website. Let's pretend that somehow it does allow people to communicate advice to their former selves. The web suffix is *dot grav* – I stumbled across it by miskeying. I've never seen a website with this ending before, but maybe it's short for *gravity*. Maybe in the future they have found a way to code information into gravity waves. Remember when they did it in that film, *Interstellar*?'

'Jesus wept!' exclaimed Martin, 'You're really taking this seriously! So you reckon if I go on the site I'll get a future *Martin Wilson* barking orders at me?'

'Well, it would be fun to find out. If it's some kind of impersonator let's see what he does to convince you that he is a future version of *yourself*. And let's see if he gives you the same wacky advice about praying, or something completely different.'

At this point I noticed that Martin had half-emptied his pint glass already. Either he was very thirsty or this conversation was making him agitated.

'So are you gonna do it?' he asked.

'Do what?' I reply.

'Pray for your own demise.'

I thought carefully. I needed to regain some credibility here; 'I suppose as a man of science I have to treat it as an experiment.'

'A man of science? I thought you served drinks at the Unicorn!'

'I mean, as a rational man who bases his ideas on evidence. Science works on the basis of making a hypothesis and then trying to disprove it, so this is what I'm trying to do. I'm trying to prove that this website is some kind of hoax and that's why I need you to help me. So will you do what I asked?'

'I said I'll do it but if anyone starts hacking me you owe me big time.'

'Agreed, but I don't think it's a hacker. It's cleverer than that. Maybe it's a new algorithm that can mimic a person based on things they've communicated online in the past, and by doing this it's able to pass itself off as an older version of that person.'

"If it is, it's not even good at it,' scoffed Martin, 'You're not remotely religious, so it's not a very good imitation of you if it's trying to get you to pray, be it normally or backwards.'

'Reverse-praying,' I corrected, 'Look, I'm just as sceptical as you, but it was you that took the lid off of all this by putting drugs in my drink, so I think it's fair for me to ask you to do this one thing to help me investigate it.'

Martin's pint was down to a quarter by now. 'I said I'm sorry for that,' stated Martin, looking down at the metal table, unable to meet my gaze. He then looked up, 'I'll open this envelope and follow the instructions when I get home. I wish I'd never tried that stupid stuff. It's sent you round the bend and if you carry on like this it's going to send me round the bend too. *Woolly Hat* can keep his new products to himself from now on.'

'Products?' I laughed, 'Is that what he calls that *snake oil* he sells you? I really don't get why you fry your brain with all that stuff. What's wrong with just having a few pints?'

'Nothing,' came the reply, 'But you're like someone who always goes on holiday to the same place because it's the only place he's ever been.'

'So come on, Mr Psychedelic, you've tried virtually everything, so why do you think that particular substance we had gives people visions that lead them to this wacky website?'

'God knows!' came the admission of intellectual defeat.

"Ha, but you don't believe in him!' I teased.

'And nor did you until you started getting those messages,' Martin fired back, 'Now you're some kind of reverse-Christian who is going to pray for bad stuff so that the opposite can happen.'

'I'm testing my hypothesis,' I reaffirmed.

'Let's test it now,' said Martin, pulling out a smartphone from his back pocket, 'What's that website again?'

'No good,' I stated firmly, 'Already tried it. The website doesn't load properly on mobile phones.'

Martin tutted, 'So I've got to do it on the computer, right?'

'Afraid so,' I concede.

With that, Martin necked down the remainder of his beer.

'Are you having another one?' I asked.

'No, I must be off, if that's all you needed me for, that is.'

'You've only been here ten minutes.'

Martin gave the impression of having had the rug pulled from under him. 'I'll get you a beer back next time. Promise,' he assured.

'No problem,' I said, 'I just fancied a bit of a catch up, that's all.'

'Another time,' said Martin, 'This has just scrambled me a bit. I need a coffee.'

'They serve it here,' I replied.

'On my own! I've got to process what I've just heard by myself. Sorry,' came the apology, 'We'll catch up soon.'

'See you,' he called across to the barmaid, who was now doing a crossword behind the bar. And with that he was gone. I remember shrugging and returning to my pint, as though this was some kind of consolation for my friend walking out on me. I had no idea whether I had presented my puzzle effectively or if I had just freaked him out. Either way I could see his back against the window outside immediately after he'd left. His movements indicated that he was opening my envelope. Curiosity had prevailed. I stared at that picture of the pack of crazed dogs chasing a poor fox across a field and took another swig.

Chapter 17

As soon as Martin was outside the Black Dog he had a burning desire to open the brown C5-sized envelope that Steven had handed to him. He stood with his back to the window and jammed his finger into a corner, slitting open one side. He pulled out the slip of paper and observed the web address, which was just that familiar long number with a weird suffix, and the question written beneath it, 'Is there something you want to tell me?'

He flicked it over, expecting there to be more writing on the reverse, but it was blank. 'Space to write the reply, I suppose,' he thought to himself, before stuffing it back into the envelope and putting it safely in the inside pocket on his black bomber jacket.

Martin walked briskly down the road, still thinking intensely about Steven's conversation. A coffee was definitely in order, maybe a nice cool iced coffee. Yes, that would do the trick and drag his mind out the mire. A kick of caffeine that you could down as fast as a milkshake.

As he stumbled towards the town centre he reached the Hummingbird Coffee Shop. 'That'll do,' he thought, and being a bit shook up he made a pig's ear of opening the door, almost falling into the place as it clattered against the wall. A group of three well-dressed women looked over from a nearby table. The oldest of the three pulled a disdainful expression. 'Bleeding snobs,' he thought to himself.

The tall young man at the counter smiled, 'Good afternoon.'

'Er, yes, hi. Could you do me an iced coffee please? Nothing fancy, just a straightforward one.'

'Yes certainly.'

Martin often wondered what women talk about when they go out together, so he listened attentively to the three women who seemed to be on some kind of office lunch. He distinctly heard one of them say 'Got a hangover I reckon.' Was she talking about him? Surely not. He'd only had one pint.

The young man put the tall glass of iced coffee down on the counter in front of Martin and he took it to a nearby table. As he sipped the cool milky beverage he relaxed for the first time and decided to take another look at Steven's slip of paper. Retrieving it from the envelope, he smoothed out the page on the table, before sitting silently staring at the web address, as though the act of observing it would somehow impart some further information to him.

Taking another slurp he felt around for the envelope to sheath the details of the mysterious website until he got home, but where was it? He must have knocked it off the table. Just then he glanced across to spot one of the women looking at the brown envelope below their table as though she was trying to hide what she was doing. 'Cheeky mare!' he thought to himself, 'Oh well, it's only a cruddy old envelope. She can have it if she wants it that badly.' And he stuffed the slip of paper into the pocket of his trousers.

The women got up to leave but the youngest of the three seemed to dawdle deliberately. She picked up the envelope that the other woman had just left on the table and walked over to him.

'I think this might be yours,' she said.

'Oh, thanks,' Martin replied in a surprised manner.

She looked nice. She was wearing a grey skirt and had a green blouse on under her long checked coat. He could smell a sweet floral perfume too.

'I'm sorry about my colleagues,' she said, 'They get a bit catty at times. Are you OK?'

'Oh gosh, is it that obvious?' stuttered Martin, 'I've just had a bit of a shock, that's all.'

'Ah right,' said Jane, 'Maybe I'll see you around.'

Was she flirting?

'What the hell!' thought Martin, reaching around in his jacket pocket for a pen. He quickly scrawled down his phone number on the envelope.

'That's my name,' he said, pointing to *Martin Wilson* on the envelope, 'And that's my number. You might be married for all I know but it was kind of you to bring this over. Give me a call if you like. Or a text. I promise I'm not a stalker. Or a drug...'

He stopped there. He was about to say 'Or a drug addict.' If she called him he realised he'd have to seriously clean up his lifestyle. And for once he'd actually have the motivation to do it.

He completed the sentence again, 'Or a druggie.' That sounded a bit less serious than 'addict.'

'I didn't think you were,' smiled Jane flirtatiously, taking the envelope. In truth, part of her motivation for approaching the dishevelled-looking man was to shock Catherine, who was always judgemental of strangers, but she thought that he looked like somebody who had got into trouble but was a decent person underneath and perhaps deserved a chance in life, a chance that maybe he'd never really been given.

And with that she was gone and Martin permitted himself to smile boldly as he looked up at a picture of a sunflower on the wall, unaware that it had been painted by the young man who had served him his iced coffee. Everyone has hidden depths.

Chapter 18 (Steven)

The next part of the story embarrasses me. I don't like to think about it. I'm going to let my ghost-writer take over for a bit. He did OK with that last chapter, so he might as well carry on.

I've given him the basic facts about what I did later that week and no doubt he'll embroider it a bit for entertainment value, but you'll see why I'm ashamed straight away. However, it's part of the story all the same, so it must be told. I'm just going to lay here for a bit. This poxy virus takes all your energy, and thinking about what happened when I was at my lowest ebb is only going to make me feel worse. Sometimes it seems like thoughts use as much energy as physical activity. Well, maybe they do. What shall I call my tale – 'The Man Who Thought Himself To Death?'

'Don't be morbid!'

'Give me a break, Anne, it's just a joke!'

Seriously though, the brain is a machine and all machines need energy to operate, so if you'll excuse me I just want to sleep now.

Chapter 19

Anybody's story is like a journey, ergo roads are like life.

The A48 through the medium-sized town of Wickersby is a case in point. It comes in, expediently bypassing the villages of Great Buckby and Little Buckby, rejoining the straight course of the old Roman road all the way to the town centre. The town's road network had never really been improved, so its commercial heart is often packed with queuing cars on this road which continues its direct course right through the centre. On the other side of town the feel is different, for the Roman course up onto the moors is far too steep for modern traffic and it is merely a footpath running from a small playing park at the edge of the suburbs, right to the top of the barren hillside.

The A48 takes a gentler route up the escarpment, with several straight sections through suburban terraced housing punctuated by sharp bends until the climb continues through trees which eventually clear as the road reaches its summit. It is here that there is a turning on the left to the small isolated church of Saint Cecilia, the grounds of which afford great views across Wickersby and a good thirty miles beyond.

Steven concluded that if he was to follow the advice of the mysterious emailer and commence a life of reverse-praying, this was to be the place to do it. He had an affinity with the place after all, for he had got married there. He knew from his recent chat with the man he knew as 'Reverend Reuben' that the smaller churches in Wickersby were always locked. He also felt that the large central church of All Saints would not be a comfortable place to kneel at an altar, praying to a god he wasn't sure he even believed in. Not with all those tourists floating around. So Saint Cecilia's it had to be.

Steven's car was over-revving as he stopped at the myriad traffic lights in the busy town centre, sluggishly following the A48 towards the hillside. As his car hit the incline, he dropped it down a gear and powered his way up each straight, with the Victorian terraces pressing in on either side, swinging around the bends so as not to lose speed, until he was climbing through a dense tunnel of trees, some of which had begin to blossom.

At the top, things were open and windswept and he turned onto the narrow driveway to the church, which ended in a small car park. There was a pathway through the little churchyard up to the dark wooden front door, where a strategically placed bench was sited for those wishing to savour the impressive view.

There was a round metal handle, and giving it a twist and pushing the door at the same time, Steven found himself inside the light airy porchway. Another door led into the church, this time with a black metal latch that he pushed to the right to release the door. Steven was now in the main part of the church, the inner sanctum, so to speak. There were rows of wooden seats, each with a red cushion in front for kneeling to pray. There was a narrow aisle down the middle, passing the pulpit and leading to the altar, beyond which was a covered table for serving communion, which was overlooked by a stained glass window.

Saint Cecilia was the patron saint of music, so it was fitting that the image in the window was of ancient people playing instruments while gazing heavenward to a glowing figure of Christ. Although Steven was in no way a religious man, he felt a certain reverence as he knelt down at the altar waiting for the words to come. He recalled how the last time he had kneeled in that spot was on his wedding day. Finally the words arrived.

"Lord, I am not a praying man and I'm not even sure what I believe, but I have to try this for my own research in hope of regaining a sense of stability. It feels wrong to pray for things that sound terrible but this I must do for the experiment to work. Please forgive me if my words are wrong."

Upon whispering these words Steven realised that he had already defied logic. If reverse-praying really worked, praying for forgiveness would mean that he would not be forgiven, but then again, if reverse-praying worked there would be nothing to forgive.

"I therefore pray that my life be cut short and that I do not live to an old age. Praying these words goes against all my instincts, even for a man of little or no faith, but I believe that the outcome is the important thing here, so let me die before my time is rightly due."

Steven then realised that this was an opportunity to reverse-pray for a number of things that could help other people too.

"I would also like to pray for my friend, Martin, that he may be a slave to drugs for his entire life. I pray for his addiction to intensify until it affects his mental and physical health causing irreversible damage."

After a pause another thought popped into his head.

"*I pray for my own marriage too. I pray that any last vestiges of it working will be snuffed out and that I will never experience romance again, not with my wife or anybody.*"

This all felt supremely wrong, but it was surely selfish to only reverse-pray for himself and those he knew well, and it was perhaps his final prayer that sounded the most heinous of all.

"*And finally I pray for the world. I pray that the future will be harder than the past. That current trends towards the impoverishment of the majority will continue and that the wealthy will continue to amass riches for themselves and harden their hearts to ignore the plight of the masses. I pray that climate change will progress beyond the point of no return, so that the world will be filled with turbulence and suffering. I pray that humans will continue to produce more children than the planet can sustain, increasing starvation and the abundance of wars for dwindling resources. I pray for death, suffering, agony, pain, crime, selfishness, greed, murder, abuse and the ultimate pointlessness of all things. Yes, the eradication of all humans, the loss of all knowledge, a universe plunged into the meaningless darkness from which all this emerged.*"

This was becoming easier, and perhaps Steven's lack of faith was what made such terrible-sounding prayers possible for him to utter, barely inaudible under his breath, with the sibilant consonants producing a quiet echo. Steven had to mentally remind himself that he was doing this so that the opposite would be true and that his intentions were what mattered, not the literal interpretation of the words which were surely the most awful words that had ever been uttered in this place. If any deity was listening, it would be aware of that.

Concluding with a reverent 'amen,' Steven rose to his feet and stood, transfixed by the stained glass window and the peacefulness of the location. He could hear the sound of birdsong outside and the low rumble of cars passing by on the A48 at the end of the drive. He felt serene. Were the reverse-prayers having an effect on his mental health already? No, that was silly. He didn't believe in this stuff anyway. It was just an experiment, wasn't it?

He walked slowly down the aisle and turned towards the inner door, which he had left ajar, but suddenly he felt overwhelmed by everything around him – the stained glass window, the intricate stonework, the framed tables of commandments on the wall, the wooden beams across the ceiling. He doubted himself. He had petitioned an all-powerful being for the most awful things he could imagine. In terms of evil, was he now in the same league as Hitler and Stalin? After all, they must have really believed what they were doing was for the greater good, and look at the millions that died and suffered as a result. Was he just as misguided as them to believe that his intentions mattered more than his words? Who would seriously pray for such things? He could only think of one mythical being that would do such a thing.

'I must be the devil himself,' he thought. He remembered that the website that had led him to these actions was red. That was a clue for sure. His thoughts were running wild. He had to get out.

Steven's pace quickened. He closed the door behind him, pulled the metal latch to the left to fasten it and then closed the outer door, securing it with its round handle.

He felt better. All those horrible words were sealed inside the church. They couldn't harm him, or anyone, outside. All the worst aspects of himself were safely secured behind two doors. They would fade away like the half-life of a radioactive element, gradually diminishing in their power, until they meant virtually nothing at all. Yes, that was how it was going to work.

Steven knew that there was a reason that he had done his praying in this little church. It would have been far simpler to pray in his own home, perhaps even lighting a candle and kneeling on a cushion to make some kind of ritual out of it. He had convinced himself that it would feel more real if he took himself off to this isolated place of worship, but perhaps the real reason was that after he had prayed, he could merely shut the door on it and walk away.

But then it struck him. Was all this madness just the latest incarnation of his dissociation? He felt stupid at having believed the emails or at least at having humoured them enough to carry out this ridiculous experiment. He felt that he had been a fool to himself and that he had been tricked into praying for the most dreadful things. In fact, he felt that he had been tricked into praying full stop. He hadn't sent a message to Heaven since he was a child and now he felt that he had returned to the naivety of youth. It all seemed like some kind of twisted joke, but as with the emails, there was no appearance of Derren Brown or any other TV trickster. He felt that he had done this to himself, and what could be more idiotic than that? This was madness; it had to stop.

Steven climbed back into his car, but he needed to clear his mind before attempting to make that gentle drive downhill, back into the comforting bustle of his hometown. He breathed deeply while gripping the steering wheel and staring at the tangled bushes in front of the car. This was real. He had to focus on reality; the rest of it was just a bunch of thoughts, stupid thoughts at that.

With this resolve, he turned the key, reversed out of the parking space and drove very slowly out to the main road, waiting for a gap in the traffic to pull out and almost freewheel back down into civilisation. Even his old, beaten up car wouldn't have to struggle this time. He breathed out at last.

'Never again,' he thought as he cruised down through the trees into the thirty limit and back down through the comfortingly regimented lines of Victorian terraces. As he descended towards the long central street with all its traffic lights seemingly on red he felt relief that some things never change.

'Never again!'

Chapter 20 (Steven)

I was right, wasn't I? Embarrassing, huh?

And I hadn't even reverse-prayed about the very condition that has dogged my life. I could have prayed that I would suffer with *impostor syndrome* and *dissociation* for the rest of my days, that I would be forever lost in a maze of forced behaviour, trying to behave how I think I should behave and never finding peace of mind.

But the truth is I had lost my grip of reality to such an extent that I'd completely forgotten about my normal concerns, like just getting through the day without my mask falling off. I was now caught up in an existential game of chess, considering whether my thoughts and actions were good or evil and whether or not I was mad.

I could see a certain logic behind what I had done, as for millennia people have always prayed for good things, for healing, for peace, for tolerance and for justice, yet the world seems to be more out of control than ever - the rape, the murder, the torture, the abuse, the misery, the disease, the pain, the sadism... It does indeed seem that the reverse of these collected prayers is happening, so why not? Why not pray for bad things and see if good things happen?

But then again, I don't really believe in any of this, so what was I doing?

Maybe I needed to speak to my older self for guidance. Listen to that, *my older self*, what madness! I'd probably get more sense speaking to Reverend Reuben! But like I said, I was hooked, and I went straight up to the study and fired up the computer, tapping in that now-familiar number to bring up that now-familiar website, but imagine my shock when all that came up was a message saying 'Site Not Found.'

I checked that my computer was properly connected to the Internet. It was. I deleted the cookies in 'settings' to make sure nothing was blocking my access and I typed it in again.

'Site Not Found.'

I wandered over to the window to try to find some inspiration looking outside. The magnolia tree looked magnificent with its pinky-white petals, and the sleepy street of semi-detached houses was like a scene from a developer's catalogue. It was the height of spring. I could hear the whirring of a lawnmower but it was the whirring of my mind that concerned me.

I had begun to make a common mistake in thinking that there was some kind of link between what was going on outside with what was going on inside my own head. I wondered if the very act of me going up to that church and praying for those terrible things had resulted in the website being closed down, having achieved its aim.

I needed to get hold of Martin again and find out if he'd been able to access the website. Yes, that made sense, so I grabbed my mobile phone from off the table next to the computer and called him.

'Hello,' came the reply in a questioning tone.

'Hi, it's Steven.'

'I can hear that.'

'Yeah, you OK?'

'Good mate, yes, really good.' This was unusually positive.

'I just wondered if you'd checked out that website yet.'

'Well, I did try to access it but there was naff all there. Just a blank screen saying *site not found*.'

'Hmm, I'm getting that too. It seems that the site has been taken down.'

'I don't wanna be funny, but are you sure it even existed? You know, with your *dissociation* thing?' prompted Martin.

'Well, yes, that sounds more like schizophrenia, and I don't have that, thank God. If we eliminate the possibility of someone drugging me it simply *must* have existed, but why would it be taken down now?'

'Beats me.'

'It's just that it seems like the site was taken down as soon as I acted on the information I was given. But why?'

There was a pause. 'Coincidence? Thousands of people must have used that website and if it gives out information to everyone, the moment that the site is taken down is bound to fit with *somebody's* response, and that *somebody* just happened to be you. Seriously man, forget it, it was a hoax, I'm telling you.'

'Easier said than done,' I replied, 'I don't feel good about what I've done. I prayed for some awful things, even about you.'

'Things are fine with me,' consoled Martin, 'You won't believe it, but I've got a date.'

This took me aback, 'Really?'

'Yeah, I went to the coffee shop and there was a group of women on the table next to me. I dropped that envelope you gave me and the youngest one returned it to me. I decided to try my luck, so I gave her my number, and *hey presto*, we're going to meet up. I'm seriously going to have to sort myself out. I mean, all I wanted to do before was get out of my head, but now I've got something else. I'm going to try and make a go of this.'

'Has she contacted you?' I asked.

'Yeah, she's been texting me a lot and we're going to meet up on Friday.'

'Well, I never,' I exclaimed, 'This is going to sound mad but I think you'll succeed. I think you're going to quit the drugs. Your days of being a guinea pig for *Woolly Hat* are ending.'

'Slow down mate, this isn't going to be easy.'

'No, but you're going to do it, I'm sure. You've got something to spur you on now.' I was filled with confidence. I had prayed that the opposite would happen, and just as the mystery emailer had said, this had achieved what I wanted. Martin was not going to pump his veins full of poison until he popped his clogs; he'd found a doorway to something new.

'I like your positivity,' laughed Martin, 'All I'm saying is that I'm going to try. Jane was proper nice and I don't want to mess it up while things are going well.'

'Jane,' I thought, 'Doesn't my wife have a colleague called Jane? No, there must be loads of *Janes* in Wickersby.'

'Well, well done you,' was all I could say.

"Cheers,' said Martin, 'I'll tell you something else, I'm gonna get back on the road again. I've seen a little brown hatchback for sale, cheap as chips. I'm gonna need a car if I'm going out dating.'

'Blimey, you haven't driven for, what is it – five years?'

'Yeah, about that. I've got to get out of this rut, so meeting Jane is one step, getting some wheels is another step and cutting out some of the weed and stuff out is another.'

'That's brilliant!' I said, feeling genuinely invigorated by Martin's new lease of life.

Just then, his attention returned to my own conundrum, 'Look, I'll have another go at getting on that website, but if it's gone, it's gone. I think you've got to put all this out of your mind cos it's messing you up. If I can do it, you can do it.'

'OK, I appreciate that. I'd better go now. We'll catch up soon, and good luck with your date.'

'Cheers mate. Keep in touch.'

And with that, the call was done.

I sat in the swivel chair staring vacantly at the window. What could all this mean? The idea that reverse-praying was something that could change lives was an enticing one, but also completely insane. I felt like I had been chosen to pioneer this concept and, like Martin, I now had some enthusiasm for life, but was I just losing it? One minute I had felt like the devil himself, the next like some kind of healer. And the crazy thing was I'd never had any interest in religion at all before. To me, a spirit was something you drank, a text was what you got on your phone and a font was something to do with typing.

Ha, I could even make jokes again.

Chapter 21 (Steven)

'OK, here we go,' I told myself as I got out of my car to begin another shift.

Why's it called the Unicorn? I just don't see the point. OK, I'll leave the jokes for now. It's time to step through that back door. I wonder what boisterousness will be going on in *Hell's kitchen* today.

I can hear the conversation already, 'Man U are going to beat you lot for sure. We've got a decent manager now.'

'Nah, City all the way. We're the true Manchester team and United are going down! We're gonna make your lot look like a bunch of clowns!'

I poke my head around the door. Jimmy is busy chopping up carrots with a knife that would be an illegal weapon if he carried it about outside and Terry is watching over an urn full of soup. 'Evening gents!'

'Evening Jonesy,' comes the reply. Then the football-based banter resumes with all the vacuousness that it possessed a few seconds beforehand.

I continue down the Hallway to Hell. How am I going to act today? Will the mask slip? Will they see who I really am? Right, take a deep breath. The audience are waiting.

The corridor is so dark and dingy that it really does feel like walking out onto a stage. I turn left and find myself behind the bar. 'Misery Guts,' aka the owner, is serving drinks tonight. That's unusual. Anabelle must be off and there must be nobody else to cover. He puts some money in the till and spots me taking my coat off.

'Ah, good timing,' he declares, 'We've got a bit of a surge. Can you jump straight in?'

'Yes, no problem,' I reply, 'No Anabelle tonight?'

'She'll be in later. She's in a bit of a state. Split up with her boyfriend. She needs to learn to leave her personal life at home. This is a business I'm trying to run here.'

I try not to react. The poor girl is probably a bit cut up. The tribulations of romance are particularly harsh to deal with at such a young age. But of course 'Misery Guts' was never young. I'm sure he must have been born aged fifty and bitter.

I soon settle into the usual routine of serving customers and providing the odd bit of light conversation about the beer, if they're ordering real ale that is. It often feels like I'm a cog in a machine, just being carried along, repeating the same phrases over and over, and the cog keeps turning until the machine breaks.

'Hey Jonesy, you look half asleep!' calls 'Misery Guts' from across the bar.

I glance up. Ugh, there's a queue of people at the bar now and I didn't even spot them. That's going to give him some ammo for future gripes I'm sure. The thing is, he must realise that he comes across as an old grouch. Surely he must sometimes ask himself if he is happy in life, and if the answer is 'no,' why doesn't he do something about it? But then again, maybe that's his problem, maybe he *can't* just snap out of it. It would be like expecting me to just snap out of this *impostor syndrome* thing.

Time passes and I wipe a few tables when it goes quiet. As I wipe away the circular marks from damp glasses and the odd smear from greasy chips it often feels that I am wiping away the conversations that happened there. Two people sitting at a table put some thoughts out into the universe and I am mopping them up with a damp cloth, only to wring them out into the sink, never to be seen again.

Just then the front doors flutter open and in walks Anabelle. Immediately I can see she's been crying. Her eyes look damp and they reflect the light from the bar. She's tried to make up her face the best that she can but everyone can see that she's not in a good way. Poor girl.

Then it strikes me that tonight her experience will be exactly what my experience is like every day. She'll have to go through the motions, smiling, chatting to customers, pretending that all is well on 'Planet Anabelle' when we already know that it isn't, but if I can see through her mask, can other people see through mine?

'Hello Anabelle,' I say.

'Oh, hi Steven. That's cold out there tonight.'

She's acting already. It's always good to start with a weather-related comment to feign immunity from all that life can throw at you, as though the weather is the most dramatic and exciting thing that you can comment upon.

'True,' I concur, 'It may be spring but the evenings are still pretty nippy.'

'A nip in the air,' muses Anabelle as she hangs up her black coat which is trimmed with fake fur, 'Well, I'm ready to start.'

'About bleeding time!' the owner mutters under his breath, knowing full well that we can both hear him, but then he starts acting too. 'Anabelle, good to see you, it's pretty busy tonight, can you get signed in on the till straight away?'

'Misery Guts' has a name by the way. His name is Reginald, but he's a *serious* Reginald, never a Reggie or Reg. I think my nickname suits him better. I did a better job naming him than his parents for sure!

It's a long story but he never wanted to run a pub. It was a project for his wife, and as he had a lot of money saved from his job in banking he bought it for her. Then she got cancer and died at only 51, leaving him stuck with the pub. He'd like to sell it but he's waiting for trade to pick up before he puts it on the market. He knows that if the figures don't stack up he'll end up getting less than he bought it for – it's that COVID virus you see – people got used to sitting at home during the lockdowns and just as they started to trickle back out they got walloped with this *cost of living* crisis.

Anabelle rinses her hands in the sink behind the bar and walks over to the computerised till. She's wearing a bright red dress tonight, as though she's made a conscious decision to wear something striking to divert attention from her low mood. After a few taps on the touch-screen she turns around and with a beaming smile she addresses the customers, 'What can I get for you?'

Amazing! How does she do it? So young and yet such a good actress.

Within ten minutes 'Misery Guts' announces 'Cigarette break' and disappears out the back. Who's he kidding? I doubt we will see him again before closing time. He'll leave me and Anabelle in charge for the rest of the evening and come back through at about eleven to make sure the punters are on their way out. I don't have a problem with this, of course, things are much more relaxed when he's not around. He can smoke a whole pack for all I care.

When things quieten down I notice Anabelle leaning on the till staring into space. She is deep in thought.

'Are you OK?' I venture.

'Sort of,' she replies, 'Did Reginald fill you in? I've finished with Aaron. He's such a pleb!'

'He did mention something,' I reply.

'The blabbering git! I said I needed a bit of time to compose myself after what had happened and he said that it wasn't a problem and that he'd keep it under his hat.'

I try to think of something nice to say; 'You're holding up well, considering.'

'I'm trying. I feel like I'm a flipping novelty act working here tonight.'

'It gets like that sometimes,' I say.

'Really?' She sounds incredulous, 'But you always seem on top of things – all that *beer chat* you do. The old gits love that!'

'If only you knew,' I say quietly, half to myself and half to her. I notice that one of the said 'old gits' called Arthur has sidled up to the bar, 'Watch this.'

'Evening Arthur, we've got a new ale on tonight.'

'Evening Simon,' [ugh – he never gets my name right] 'Is that that hoppy one you mentioned last time?'

'Certainly is,' I say, pouring a small sample into a glass and handing it to him, 'Light in colour, fresh tasting but with a bitter finish.'

Arthur takes a sip and then proclaims, 'Oh yeah, that's a goodun for sure.'

'It's from that new brewery – Jenkinson's.'

'Never heard of it!'

'It's a little micro-brewery out in the sticks,' I elucidate as I pour him a pint, 'The bloke was brewing in his shed for years but *Jenkinson's Gold* got more and more popular and now he employs about ten staff I think.'

'Blimey, up and coming then?'

'It seems that way.'

The old man picks up his pint as though handling a valuable prize and walks away, 'Cheers!'

I turn back to Anabelle, 'See what I mean – it's all an act!'

'You mean that's not really you?' questions my young colleague.

'Pretty much. When I first got the job here I decided to swat up on all the local breweries and beers. I thought it would be useful for making a bit of conversation with the customers. It's served me well, as nobody has found out that it's all a charade in eight years.'

'Nobody except me,' smiles Anabelle. She looks visibly happier and that makes me feel good. It seems that my evening at the Unicorn has served a purpose beyond getting the glasses of fluid from the pumps and into the nicotine-stained hands of old men.

Anabelle then seems to open up like a book, 'I wish Aaron had been more like you. He was so full of himself, posing about in that BMW, always looking in the mirror, he'd even taken up golf because he'd heard it's what people with money did. It was as though I never really knew him because he was too busy being somebody he's not.'

'I'll take that as a compliment,' I joke, trying to keep a healthy level of detachment.

'Can I speak to you outside at the end of the night about something?' she then asks quietly.

'No worries,' I agree. I'm guessing she wants to let off steam about her break-up. I can't imagine her parents wanting to listen much about it so maybe I can serve a function there too.

Eleven o'clock soon comes around and a booming voice blasts out from behind me, 'Last orders!'

Jesus! I wish he wouldn't do that. He disappears for hours and then sneaks in and booms out like a town crier from behind you. A rush of people arrive at the bar, some necking down half of their drink as they walk. Anabelle and I serve them while 'Misery Guts' potters around at the back of the bar. I have no idea what he's doing. Probably not much.

Before long the hubbub of chatter fades as the customers sup up and drift away into the night. Arthur is the last one left. 'That's a damn good beer!' he declares as he puts his empty glass on the bar, 'Night all.'

'Goodnight,' the three of us reply in unison, with varying levels of earnestness.

'Right, that's all folks!' announces the owner, 'Same time tomorrow.'

'Another day, another half a dollar,' I answer, while Anabelle just opts for an unenthusiastic 'see ya.'

With our coats donned, the owner holds open the door as the pair of us depart.

'Go easy,' he says as he closes and locks the door.

Anabelle reaches into her pocket and pulls out a pink vaping stick. 'You know I said I wanted a word?' she ventures.

'Yep,' I reply coolly, 'Is is about Aaron?'

'Kind of, well, not really. You see the reason I split up with Aaron is that I like somebody else, but it's stupid because this other person is married, but if I've got that person in my head it's not right to keep Aaron stringing along, is it? Everything he does just seems to annoy me now.'

'Well,' I begin slowly, as she breathes a plume of vapour into the air, 'Feelings come and go. You might like this new person now, but if you avoid whoever it is the feelings should ease off. That way you'll be able to see Aaron as he really is and work out if you like him or not.'

'Look at me. Steven Jones – the agony uncle!' I think to myself.

'Well, it's not so easy, I see this person nearly every day. The trouble is Aaron just seems so superficial and childish compared to the other guy.'

'Well, it's a guy then,' I deduce, feeling like a detective trying to solve a case. I know very little about Anabelle; she could be bi for all I know. 'I think you're very mature for 22,' I compliment her, 'Maybe Aaron has got a bit of catching up to do, but he will catch up in the end I'm sure.'

'Too late for that. I told him to bog off!' she laughs. Her bluntness makes me chuckle. She inhales a deep drag of strawberry-flavoured nicotine, as though it is some kind of fuel that is going to power her through what she's about to say. The trail of vapour comes out with the words, 'I think when you've got something in your head that's driving you mad you should just let it out, for better or for worse, right?'

'I suppose so,' I respond, although I've no idea where this is going.

'Well, it could be for worse as we'll still have to work together.'

Oh God! I can see where this is heading...

'I've been working with you for a couple of years but for a few weeks now I've started to feel differently...'

'Anabelle,' I interject, hoping to stall her before she embarrasses herself, but she continues.

'I know it's crazy, but when I saw you chatting with your friend the other week I started seeing a different side of you. I thought "He's not just the guy who rambles on about the beer, but he's really trying to help his friend here."'

'Oh Martin,' I say dismissively, 'Anabelle, I think you...' but she cuts in again. She's clearly reiterating a rehearsed speech.

'Then I started chatting with you a bit more and it was so much different to chatting to Aaron. Aaron's not really interested in anything other than himself and how he looks to his friends, but you don't seem to give a monkey's, and I thought "I want to be with someone like that." So really, what I'm saying is, I know you're married and I know it's not going well because you said so, so why shouldn't we get to know each other? Why shouldn't we have a bit of romance? Life's too short!'

I open my mouth, unsure of what is going to tumble out; I just hope it's the right thing. 'I take it you know how old I am?'

'Yeah, 37!' She's done her research.

'And that doesn't bother you?' I enquire.

'Not really. The lads my age are all jerks.'

'Eloquent,' I think to myself.

'They can't all be like that,' I say, 'But the truth is I'm very flattered and you look stunning. If I was in my twenties I'd jump at the chance but my life is very complicated. I've got a wife and I've no idea if it's over or not, plus I've got a load of other stuff I'm dealing with which is really doing my head in.'

'Well, I'll always listen,' says Anabelle kindly.

'Thank you. It's just that I struggle to get through my shifts at work and if there's another element of awkwardness because we're having some kind of relationship, I'm not sure I could deal with it all. There's something else going on as well and if I explained it you probably wouldn't want to know me at all; you'd think it's madness. But I need to get to the bottom of this madness before I can work out what's going on at home and whether or not I want another relationship, no relationship, my wife's relationship or whatever.'

'I get it,' Anabelle concedes, 'I don't think I could find anything you say to me *madness* though, just *interesting*.'

Why is she being so nice? It's not making this any easier. I then remember part of what I'd prayed up at Saint Cecilia's. *No romance ever again*, remember?

'The thing is, even this conversation we're having now is part of the conundrum. I think I've discovered something where the opposite of things I think seems to happen. It happened with my friend Martin and it's happening again now.'

'But how did you discover something like that? Life is just random things happening, surely?'

'Is it?' I reply rhetorically, trying to sound in control of what I'm saying, 'So if I said I was getting messages through a website that nobody else can seem to access, what would you think?'

'It's weird but I don't think you're crazy!'

Stop being so nice!
'...And that I discovered the website because somebody spiked my drink and sent me on some kind of acid trip or something.'
'Yikes! That's heavy.'
We have breakthrough!
But then she comes back again, 'It was that mate of yours, wasn't it? We all know that he smokes weird stuff. Reginald said "If I ever catch him doing it here he's barred!" And yet, you tried to help him. You're a good person, Steven. I'm sick of all the bad lads and all their posing.'
'I can't say I'm a fan of them either,' I joke, stalling for time, 'Look, let's take what the Americans call a rain check on this. I've heard what you've said and it's very nice. I won't be any different to usual with you at work so there won't be any discomfort, but I need to clear my mind and sort out this mess. Then I can think clearly and decide if it's a good idea for us to meet outside of work or not. The truth is, I'd love to, but even though things are messed up with Anne at home I'm not sure I could live with myself if I did something rash without the marriage being properly over. I have memories too, you see, going back to the early days when I met her – maybe like you and Aaron – so to just bin all that without really knowing what I'm doing could be unforgivable, not because of Anne, but because of being true to myself.'
'Wow, that was deep!' exclaimed Anabelle, sliding the vape stick back into the pocket inside her coat, 'So where do we go from here?'
I look up at the night sky. A few stars are managing to twinkle through the streetlight haze of the town. I can think of nothing more to say.
'Home, I guess.'

Chapter 22

'Something's going on!' declared Anne as the three colleagues sat down at their usual table in the Hummingbird Coffee Shop.

'What do you mean?' asked Catherine, 'What's going on?'

'It's Steven, he's up to no good!'

'Drugs?' asked Catherine as respectfully as possible.

'No, not drugs,' Anne replied dismissively, 'He's got another woman. I'm sure of it.'

Three tea plates and a larger plate with three chocolate eclairs upon it was brought over to the table by the tall young waiter, who had hidden talents as an artist.

'Thank you, Jacob' said Jane, remembering that the staff were human too and didn't deserve to be ignored and having recently taken the time to ask his name.

'No worries,' acknowledged Jacob.

Anne continued, 'I had a peep in his latest diary the other night and I'll show you what it says on my phone.' Biting into their eclairs and wiping the cream from their mouths with napkins, Anne's two colleagues lent forward to read the screen-shot on Anne's phone.

'Really weird night at work. A. was late due to trauma so I had to work with the boss. Had nice chat and it cheered her up but she revealed something that made me question my whole life. Have I made the right decisions? Too much confusion. Wish it would all go away. Why did I pray for no romance at Saint Cecilia's? Should have been more careful. I meant long term, not ASAP. Still can't believe this is happening.'

Jane was the first to respond, 'Hang about. I don't think it means what you think it means. There must be an explanation.'

'Always seeing the good in people,' laughed Catherine, 'Men are swines!'

'Thanks for that piece of enlightenment,' chirped the youngest of the three women sarcastically, 'So who is *A*?'

'If it's who I think it is, it's that dappy girl he works with, Anabelle. He's always on about her. Anabelle this, Anabelle that. He must realise how obvious it is. Look at it logically. He's obviously started something with her and he's prayed for the romance to stop because he hasn't got the gumption to just say no. Then through sheer coincidence it *has* stopped and now he doesn't like it. He wanted it to last longer, but not long enough for me to find out what's going on.'

'No, not Steven, it can't be,' sympathised Jane, 'I thought you said he's not even religious so what's all the praying about?'

'He's gone crazy, I told you,' remonstrated Anne, 'The drugs have twisted his mind. He probably thinks he's got a direct line to God or something.'

'My Matt is OK, but I gave up trying to understand blokes years ago,' chipped in Catherine, 'You'll tie yourself up in knots trying to make sense of things. If it bothers you, just confront him.'

'But how? I can't just say I've been snooping about in his box of books.'

'Catch 22,' mused Jane.

'22, you're right there, that's how old she is and she's his catch. Just a slip of a girl!'

'Who does he think he is, Peter Stringfellow?' joked Catherine.

'I still don't believe it,' stated Jane emphatically, 'There must be an explanation, but often the explanations are so complicated that you could never guess the truth.'

'You're not wrong there,' agreed Anne, 'So one of you says *affair* and one of you says *no way.*' There was a moment of silence and the three ladies all picked up their cups in unison, taking a swig.

'Where's Saint Cecilia's anyway?' asked Catherine thoughtfully.

'It's that church up on the moors. We got married there. It's nice in summer but chilly and windswept the rest of the year. God knows why he goes up there. There are plenty of closer churches if he's got religion.'

'Patron saint of music,' remarked Jane. The other two looked confused so she elaborated, 'Saint Cecilia.'

'And what's music the food of?' posed Catherine provocatively, 'It's probably where he meets her. It's out of the way, it's quiet and there's no chance of you popping up there and catching him.'

'Are you crazy?' defended Jane, 'In a church?'

'He's not religious, remember?' replied Catherine smugly.

'Look, this is still my husband we're talking about,' rebuked Anne, 'I wanted to get your thoughts on it, not play word games.'

'Yes, sorry,' apologised Catherine, 'I get a bit carried away. I've just had so much bad luck with men that I always think the same.'

Jane was swift to chip in, 'Maybe that's *why* you have so much bad luck. You're expecting the worst so it happens.'

'Just because you've got some fancy man!' came the reply.

Anne clattered her teacup back into the saucer, 'Jane Mitchell!'

'Yes, that's my name.'

'You never mentioned this.'

'I'm not shouting it from the rooftops if that's what you mean. It's early days so we'll just see how it goes. Not a word about this at work, ladies.'

'OK, mum's the word, but keep us posted.'

'Not good enough,' said Catherine, 'We'll keep it quiet, but what's he like? Is he young, old, rich, poor, thin, fat...?'

Jane braced herself. There was only one way to put a stop to this gossip. 'If you must know it's that chap that came into the coffee shop the other week. He nearly took the door off its hinges, remember?'

Anne's teacup came clattering back into the saucer again, this time accompanied by a dribble of tea that had found its way to freedom through her open mouth. 'Tell me you are having a laugh!'

'No, he's a nice guy. He looked a bit rough that time but he'd had a bad day. He scrubs up pretty well.'

Catherine just tutted and rolled her eyes.

'Do you know who that is?' asked Anne assertively.

'Martin Wilson, the last time I asked.'

'Yes, Martin Wilson, also known as Steven's friend Martin, the druggie.'

'Oh my!' remarked Jane, 'He said he'd had a few issues with addiction and that he was determined to clean himself up. Well, all power to his elbows, that's what I say. Everyone deserves a second chance.'

'But...' stuttered Anne, 'He's the one who spiked Steven's drink.'

'Come off it!' laughed Jane, 'He's not that kind of guy.'

'Ha!' scoffed Anne, 'Before you know it you'll be off your trolley on magic mushrooms, and you won't even know it. He'll probably sneak a few into a paella or something.'

'I'm keeping out of this one,' said Catherine, polishing off her chocolate eclair and glancing out of the window as a mother pushed a pushchair along the pavement outside.

'Do you really think he'll be able to knock the drugs on the head?'

Jane had faith, 'Yes I do.'

'I hope you're right,' answered Anne charitably, 'I just don't want you to be disappointed. The addict is like a bottomless pit. He's empty inside and he throws drugs into the hole, hoping that the hole will fill up, but the hole never fills up because it's bottomless.'

'Here we go,' remarked Catherine, 'Anne and Jane's philosophy hour again.'

'I don't think Martin's problems are any different to any other kind of addiction,' defended Jane, 'Look at Old Man Jessop, he's got all the money he could ever wish for. He could retire today and live in luxury, but no, he has to carry on. He's never satisfied because he's a bottomless pit, just like all fat cat bosses. I'm not jealous of them; I pity them, because they can never be satisfied.'

Anne brought the conversation back down to earth. 'But you're not going out with money-addict Mr Jessop; you're going out with drug-addict Mr Wilson.'

Jane decided to remain silent and joined Catherine in staring out of the window. A black cab went past and this seemed to stir her into animation. '...And anyway, if Martin is a friend of Steven's maybe I can do a bit of scouting around for you. Blokes always chat just like we do. I bet Martin knows what's going on with Steven, if anything is going on at all, that is.'

'That's true,' said Anne quietly, and suddenly her disapproval of Jane's new relationship seemed to soften, 'Would you be willing to do that then?'

'I don't see why not,' came the reply, 'But it's on one condition.'

Anne looked inquisitively.

'...That you butt out of judging Martin and let me decide for myself.'

Chapter 23 (Steven)

This is so dull, laying here reflecting over the last few weeks, simply because I lack the energy to carry on with my normal life at the moment. It's one of those 'be careful what you wish for' situations. For years I've wished that I didn't have to go to work and endure this ordeal of pretending to be me, but now that wish has actually been granted I'd do anything to get out of this house and chat about beer and breweries to customers, pour a few pints and have a chin-wag with Anabelle. Ah yes, Anabelle, you're probably wondering what happened next.

Well, I was very confused when I got home from work that night and it was a struggle to dismiss all the 'what ifs' from my mind. What if I actually did meet Anabelle for a drink? That wouldn't be infidelity, would it? But then, my intentions wouldn't be purely innocent, so maybe it would constitute infidelity after all. It was a moral maze, but one that I couldn't stop thinking about. Was this the opportunity to escape from my mundane life that I had been waiting for? Or was it just a further stultifying layer of confusion to add to the mix, like mist sitting on top of mist, pushing down, denser and denser?

Anne was upstairs asleep and I sat on the settee staring at a blank TV screen, wondering if any of the recent events really had anything to do with my act of reverse-praying at the church. I'd prayed that Martin would be addicted to drugs for the rest of his life, and there he was, cleaning himself up and giving himself a second chance, all because of a random meeting with a young lady. I'd also prayed that I wouldn't experience romance ever again, with my wife or with anybody else, and now here was this attractive young girl virtually offering herself to me on a plate! Even in these days of equality it seems that the man always has to be the one to take the gamble and ask the woman out – not the other way round – but here was Anabelle asking *me*!

But these weren't the only things I'd prayed for. I'd prayed for endless war, greed and environmental destruction, and that's pretty much how things have continued, not the opposite. Maybe the difference was that I didn't actually believe it was possible for God to intervene on a global scale. Maybe that's why reverse-praying worked for Martin and myself but not for the entire planet. At least not so far.

I wanted to test the theory out further, but I also wanted some peace of mind. My nights were becoming less and less occupied with sleep and more and more dominated by deep yet aimless thought. I would return to the church the next day before work and send up another reverse-supplication. Yes, that was the only solution. With this resolve I climbed the stairs to join Anne in slumber, but I had another one of those wacky dreams that night.

"I don't know if I was homeless but it was Christmas and I wanted to contribute to the family meal. I had a small grilling machine outside our house and there was a big slice of pork fat that Anne had thrown outside. I decided to cook it and crispen it up into a nice piece of crackling. I was sitting down on the pavement beneath the magnolia tree, which was of course bare in winter, and the grill was on the pavement in front of me. The next minute I was back in the house and I'd got greasy rust-coloured fat all over the carpet and it had caught fire.

I got some carpet cleaning fluid and a bucket of water which I tipped over the flames to extinguish them. The fire had charred the carpet and I was scrubbing away with the cleaning fluid, hopelessly trying to return it to its former glory, but the singed threads were coming off with every rub of the cloth until it was just a bare mesh with no pile on it at all.

It was then that a young man came in. This was Aaron, Anabelle's boyfriend. I have no idea what he looks like in reality, but in the dream he was a cocky chap in a black leather jacket. He stared down at the carpet as though he was disgusted and I suddenly felt an intense dislike for him. He had no idea that I had been trying to do the right thing and that it was purely by accident that I had made the carpet worse. How dare he come into my former house, assuming that I was now some kind of vagrant, and start giving me disparaging looks about the damage I'd done to my own carpet. I was furious and I lunged at him, knocking him into the cabinet in the living room with Anne's porcelain dolls in. He fell over backwards and the glass doors smashed. Porcelain flew everywhere and the dolls shattered into pieces.

At the end of the dream I was scooping the debris into a pile in the middle of the room, pushing the broken glass and porcelain into the heap with my feet. It was just like the other dream with the broken chairs and tables, and suddenly I realised that I was in a dream."

I woke up with a start. It was 3.06am. 'Why is there so much anger in my dreams?' I wondered to myself, convinced that the trauma must be trying to communicate something to me, 'And fire, why is there always fire?'

I do believe that the subconscious is often ahead of the curve. It gives warnings in dreams when trauma is present but as yet undetected. Just what did the smashed porcelain dolls mean? Were the actions I was toying with going to smash up people's lives as surely as those dolls?

I remembered that I had resolved to go to Saint Cecilia's and sort this mess out. Maybe I was searching for the Superglue from my other dream – the glue that would stick all these shattered pieces and fragmented thoughts back together. Why did I have children in the other dream? Did I think that Anne and I could have held on to our marriage longer if we'd had some?

I slept well for the rest of the night, not stirring until Anne was getting up, ready for another day of riveting excitement at Jessop and Davies Accountancy. I snoozed on for a while, but if I dreamed anything else I don't remember it. The next thing I knew I heard the front door clunk shut and Anne was on her way. This seemed a good time to get up.

There was a thick mist outside and I stared into the haze through the kitchen window as though divining it for answers as I consumed my tea and toast. Without further ado, I grabbed my long brown coat from the peg in the hall and headed for the car. I was going to Saint Cecilia's.

Now the truth is, I get a bit embarrassed about these religious bits, as I'm not sure what I even believe. A few weeks ago I would have said 'I believe in nothing at all' but now I just prefer to keep quiet about it, so I'm going to let my ghost-writer take over again. He didn't make a total hash of it last time, so I'm trusting him to relate what happened next as clearly and as truthfully as possible.

Chapter 24

Getting through the town centre at that time of day wasn't too much of an ordeal, with rush hour long over and the lunchtime hustle still a couple of hours away. The A48 led Steven up out of suburbs, swinging around those sharp bends into each long straight hemmed in by red-bricked Victorian terraces. Then it was up through the blossoming trees and out onto the windy plain at the top of the ridge.

Steven turned left into the driveway to the church and pulled into the little car park, with its row of densely knotted bushes obscuring the quite spectacular view across the town beyond. Steven had sat staring at those bushes as he tried to gather his thoughts after that first visit, a visit which had made him feel like he was the very devil himself. Today they seemed gentler, with some green leaves beginning to soften their appearance.

Steven left the womb of his car and wandered up the gently curving path towards the imposing wooden door into the porchway of the little stone church. He jiggled the various clasps and handles to open both doors, and once inside, it immediately felt like a second home. The church no longer seemed like a foreboding place where he didn't belong; this time it seemed natural to be there and Steven savoured the peace of the gentle breeze rustling the young leaves outside and the call of the ubiquitous wood pigeons.

He was on a mission though, and no sooner had he entered than he found himself heading straight for the altar which was bounded by a flimsy wooden rail. Steven was there to do one thing and one thing only, so after gazing reverently at the stained glass window behind the altar, he dropped to his knees. The first time he had done this he had felt self-conscious and silly, but this time he felt like a seasoned churchgoer. Then in a whispered tone, the words began to spill out.

"Forgive me for a second supplication and for the unnatural words I am about to utter. If you are truly there, you know that my intentions are good and that it is just my words that sound evil and not my heart, but with this in mind I pray the following.

"I repeat my prayers for the world to be full of suffering, war and violence, and for humans to continue to destroy the planet that sustains them. I pray for evil to triumph and good to cower in the face of the brute force of money. I pray for cruelty to animals,

cruelty to children and a world where arrogance and vanity will rip apart all that is good. But I realise that when I am praying for the whole world my belief is weak, so it is for myself that I must pray now.

"My mind is awash with thoughts as a result of these prayer experiments and I pray that my confusion will multiply. I pray that my life will become even more intense, intolerably intense in fact, so that I feel stressed and anxious to the point where I risk a nervous breakdown. I pray that I will get no rest from my own chattering mind. I pray that my thoughts will drive me insane and that I will experience complete burnout. I pray that my thoughts will multiply uncontrollably like cancer cells, until my mind is taken over by the sheer madness of it."

Concluding reverently with an 'Amen,' Steven rose to his feet. 'That ought to do the trick,' he thought to himself, and he bowed respectfully before the stained glass window, as though this action might neutralise the terrible-sounding prayer. He gazed around the church trying to take in the atmosphere; this really was such a peaceful spot. There was an old wooden pulpit with a few steps up to where the preacher would deliver his sermon and red cushions for kneeling upon in front of each wooden chair, the chairs being arranged in regimented rows either side of the aisle.

Steven decided that this time he would sign the visitors' book which was bound in black leather, or maybe black PVC. He wrote the day's date, put his name as Steven Jones and his location as Wickersby, with the simple comment 'peaceful' after it. He flicked through the names and comments, curious at what other people had written. Nothing truly stood out or grabbed his attention. 'Boring lot!' he thought.

At this point I am tempted to write that he flicked through and saw his own name signed in shaky handwriting and dated around forty years later than the present date, indicating that the mystery emailer was indeed an older version of himself and that his presence was felt inside the church, but no, what makes for an interesting story isn't always as compelling as the truth. Steven merely strolled out of the church, fastening the doors behind him.

Turning around outside the porch, he was struck by an awe-inspiring view, for the mist was now entirely below the line of the hills and the sky above was a deep blue with the sun beating down.

He could see nothing of Wickersby town or the surrounding countryside beneath the dense white shroud. It felt similar to looking down on the clouds from the window of a plane. The air felt clean and fresh, as though whatever entity Steven had just prayed to had forgiven his words and was smiling upon him now.

He wandered back to his car, transfixed by the view until that line of green leafy bushes obscured it once again, and as he took his place at the driver's seat he examined his thoughts once more. This time there was none of the angst that he felt after his first visit, for he was certain that he had taken this experiment as far as it could go. If reverse-praying worked, he would find his life calming down, his thoughts would be pacified and he would clamber his way out of the moral maze that he had become embroiled in. Conversely, if reverse-praying was just total nonsense being proffered by a crank pretending to be his future self, things would probably just carry on the same, but even so, would this not also mean that he had an answer? Either way, he'd be able to get on with his life and accept the direction in which it was headed.

Steven felt at peace and he concluded that perhaps a clear mind was the greatest blessing of all, and one that many people take for granted. He savoured the moment before turning the key in the ignition once again.

Chapter 25 (Steven)

As I drove back down that hill into Wickersby I felt curiously tired. This didn't make sense; it was 11am and I was usually at my peak around this time of day. I yawned profusely and almost had to pull over as I didn't feel safe driving.

I came down through the terraces into the town centre and negotiated my way along the dead-straight central street through to the opposite side of the town where I live. Pulling into the leafy suburb I had just one desire – to get straight into bed and to sleep it off.

I locked the car up on the drive and stumbled into the magnolia tree, sending a flurry of browned petals to the ground around me. It had passed its peak and its triumphant display of colour had begun to tarnish. After fumbling with my key in the lock, I crashed through the front door and headed straight for the stairs. The tiredness completely overwhelmed me. I felt ill but I couldn't put my finger on it, but then I realised, I must have picked up that poxy virus.

I climbed into bed fully clothed and pulled the quilt over myself. I felt chilly, which was ridiculous. The mist outside had cleared and made way for a lovely spring day with temperatures in the high teens, but there I was, laying there shivering. I really couldn't see myself going to work that day, so I decided to call in sick. Thankfully it was Anabelle who answered the phone and not 'Misery Guts.' She was doing the lunchtime shift. I asked if she could pass a message on that I was ill and that I suspected COVID. I'd do a lateral flow test as soon as I could but I'd have to wait until Anne could get me some from the chemist as I was drained of energy.

She said that she would pass the message on for me and I concluded the call by meekly asking 'Are you OK?'

'I'm fine,' she replied, 'Hope I didn't freak you out last night. I just blurt things out sometimes.'

'I think I freaked myself out,' I replied, 'Thinking about all this crazy stuff, but if I've got this virus now I guess that will give me time to chill out a bit.'

'Well, maybe,' came the answer, 'You could be off for a long time if you've got coronavirus. Maybe it will be good for us both to clear our heads.'

'That's true. I hate laying in bed though. I need a project.'

'Well, I reckon you've got a story to tell. Why not write a

book?' encouraged Anabelle.

'I haven't really got the language skills for that. I'd need a ghost-writer to tidy it up for sure. It could be cathartic, mind you.'

'Listen to yourself,' laughed Anabelle, 'Cathartic! And you say you haven't got the language skills! You'll be telling me it's getting crepuscular outside next!'

'Ha, good word but it's ages till evening,' I chuckled, but Anabelle was serious about this book idea.

'Anyway,' she added, 'There's a bloke who comes in occasionally who writes novels. I reckon he'd have a look at it.'

'I just need to sleep at the mo,' was my low-energy reply.

'OK, I'll tell Reginald you're sick. And get well soon.'

'Thanks Anabelle.'

I dropped the phone onto the bedside table and I must have been asleep in seconds. It was a deep dreamless sleep and when I woke up it was 5pm. I was boiling hot and sweating all over, so I threw back the quilt, removed my jumper and turned on the fan by the bed. As I lay there in the circulating air I felt zombie-like, and when I looked back on the morning's visit to the church on the hill it seemed like a dream, as though I wasn't sure if it had actually happened or not.

This was reality now. My muscles ached and I didn't even have the motivation to get up and pour myself a glass of water. Anne would be home soon, and although our marriage was as dry as the Sahara Desert, she wouldn't hesitate to help if I was ill.

As I stared at the clouds drifting slowly behind the roofs through the window it did feel as though the brakes had been put on my life. I had questions, but they weren't the kind of intense questions that I'd had before – the kind of questions that demanded instant answers. I just passively mused that perhaps I had reverse-prayed my way into contracting this virus. I had asked for uncontrollable thoughts to push me ever-closer to a nervous breakdown and I received 'laying in bed, peacefully watching fluffy white clouds sailing past suburbia.' If that's not reverse-praying I don't know what is.

So this brings us up to date. I've been in and out of this bed for a few weeks now, shuffling downstairs to make cups of tea and returning to this room like a slow-motion boomerang each time. They think it might be long COVID. Well, I just long to get rid of it now! Anne has been very good and she has slept in the spare room ever since I went down with it. She's managed to escape the dreaded lurgy so far. She brings me food and I can rest as much as I like. Even 'Misery Guts' has been fairly understanding. I expect Anabelle has had a hell of a time with him behind the bar doing my duties, but it's not wise for me to keep thinking about her, is it? That ship has sailed – I wanted the nuclear bomb of my life diffused and now that wish has been granted. If 'bland' is your thing, this is the lifestyle for you!

So during my waking hours I've been scrawling down a few notes. If Anabelle can get hold of that author, he'll be able to tidy them up and thrash it into shape a bit. I keep the notepad under the mattress. It's not for Anne's eyes, you see. Obviously, if it's published she'll get to see it, but if there are any bits she doesn't like I can just say that the ghost-writer pepped it up a bit. Simple, hey?

Here, see what you think. If I can just lean over enough to pull it out from beneath the mattress I'll give you a taster.

Ah, there we go. Now, where were we? I need to flick through this. Hmm, that's just a shopping list, some doodles... Right, here's the opening paragraph:

"Laying on your back 24-7 may be a cure for some minds and a cancer for others. It all depends if your life is something that needs to be cured or if it is a finely-tuned engine of pleasure.

"I suppose I had better introduce myself. My name is Steven Jones. It's a stupid name. Say it over and over again, go on, keep repeating it. It sounds stupid, right? And anyway, how can three syllables sum up what a person is, not just at this current moment in time but at all moments in time, forever? That's why I don't like names. How can you put a name on a person when a person isn't even the same from one year to the next?

"So what am I doing here?

"Well, it's that stupid virus, right..."

Chapter 26 (Steven)

I've been thinking. It's not a popular hobby these days, I know, but when you're stuck indoors like this you can do little else and I've been told by the doctor to stay inside for at least another week. It's 'death by boredom' for sure.

Do you remember that number that Martin hallucinated that led me to the website that got me into this whole weird situation? Two to the power of twenty? Well, I've been wondering if I can find more sites with the same suffix by trying different powers of two. The obvious one would be 'two to the power of thirty' I guess. I'm still not really sure if I believe any of what happened to me. Was it all just a series of bizarre coincidences? Was the *unreality* of my mental state making me perceive things inaccurately? I don't know.

When recalling something that has happened you can never be sure if it really happened at all, for the mind recreates memories afresh every time you recall them. This is why two people can have completely different recollections of the same event. Each of their brains is putting its own spin on things. In short, how can we be sure that anything we remember ever actually occurred?

Well, this seems the easiest way for me to deal with it now. If I really believe that I received a hallucinogenic vision of the same number as Martin which led me to a website where a future version of myself advised me to reverse-pray and this had turned out to be a foolproof way to get what you want, I'd be packaged off to the funny farm for sure. It's simpler just to rationalise it as a manifestation of the *dissociation* problem that I have. Derealisation, depersonalisation, dissociation, call it what you want. As I said at the start, what's in a name anyway?

So you now find me sitting in front of the computer with a notepad. I've just been doubling powers of two. I could use a calculator if I wanted to, but I've got so much time that I tend to do tasks in more complex ways these days, just to keep my mind active and kill extra minutes. At present, my life feels like crawling across the Sahara Desert with no idea how much further I have to go. Getting well again could be just over that next dune, or it could be way past the horizon beyond.

I gaze down at the notepad. At the bottom of a slowly expanding column of figures I've written 1,073,741,824. If we were dealing with computing, and we are in a way, this would represent a *gibibyte*, not a *gigabyte* as is often misconceived, but do you care?

I tap the figure into the search box, making sure that all the digits are correct, and I type the 'dot grav' suffix. A page loads on the screen which looks a bit like one of those boxes of black and white squares that you scan with your phone – a QR code – that's what its called! The only thing is, this image fills the entire screen and it's my own eyes, and not my phone, that are scanning it.

I stare into the complex image in front of me and it seems to gain depth. Remember those 'magic eye' images that were popular, where if you stare at a pattern long enough it looks 3D? Well, it's a bit like that, but it feels very odd, as if it's doing something to my mind. I feel transfixed by it but I don't know why. It's as though I am becoming immersed in what is on the screen. 'Am I having one of my dissociative episodes?' I wonder.

Now 'QR' stands for 'quick response,' but there's nothing quick happening here as I stare meditatively at the image, as though trying to hypnotise myself with it. Perhaps I'm trying to subconsciously extract whatever meaning is contained within that code. It's no use, my eyes are becoming blurry, I'll have to look away.

Woah, I wasn't expecting that! I gaze around me and the mass of black and white squares is everywhere now. It's as though everything I look at has become pixelated. If I move my head, the position of the squares changes in relation to me. It's like I'm in a coded version of reality. I can feel that I am still sitting on that familiar swivel chair at my desk, but my entire world is composed of the same coded image. Has staring at that code hacked into my brain somehow?

I wonder if I'm having one of those dreams that I've been getting lately. Maybe I fell asleep in the chair and drifted into a dreamworld without noticing the point where reality ended and my mind began. But how is it going to end? Am I going to fly into a rage and release all that repressed subconscious angst that seems to come out in my night-time visions?

There is a cup of coffee next to the keyboard on the desk. Like everything else it appears to consist entirely of black and white squares. I can see where the handle is and I reach for it. However, there was more coffee in it than I thought and some of it splashes out onto the desk, or should I say that I saw a blob of the QR code moving from the mug to the desk.

In spite of the bizarreness of this experience, I feel calm. It's not like when I was running along the road after Martin spiked my drink, it feels more like a revelation, maybe I am seeing the world as it really is – just a mass of code. Perhaps I'm living in a simulation.

Now, if that was true, that feeling that I've always had where I am real and the world around me is not makes perfect sense. I'm not dissociated at all, for the world really is just a construction – I'm the one that is real – the only one! But then it often feels like I am the one who isn't real; it's me who feels like he's always acting after all.

Bizarrely, I feel no need to panic. If I am dreaming I just need to sit it out until I wake up. Likewise, if I'm having a dissociated episode I know that they don't last for ever. Eventually I'll be 'back to reality' to quote from a 1980s song that Martin probably has in his collection. I can't understand how this experience, which logically should be frightening, actually feels fine, relaxing even. But where is it leading me? Am I in transit between two worlds as we speak?

I think the best thing I can do is close my eyes and relax. I can still feel the swivel chair beneath me so I know I'm safe, but if I close my eyes, maybe when I open them I'll have completed my journey.

So I sit and stare at the back of my closed eyelids. Dots flash before me but they're familiar, I've seen these coloured dots before. They're not unusual. I guess the brain needs something visual to process when there's nothing coming towards it along the optic nerve, so 'dots' it is!

I just sit, waiting.

Waiting.

Interminably waiting.

Chapter 27

The Hummingbird Coffee Shop was extraordinarily busy. Not only were the tables all full but people were leaning against various shelves drinking their beverages.

'What's going on? It's not payday is it?' Jane had asked when they first sat down with their hot drinks and baguettes.

'No, we've ages until Old Man Jessop opens his wallet again,' replied Catherine, 'But I've never seen it like this in here before, not even on pay day.'

A short time later they had cleared their plates and the young waiter brought over a small plate with a fruit tart which Anne had ordered when buying a second drink. There were cherries in a thick red syrup and a dollop of cream on top.

'Thanks, that looks delicious,' Anne declared.

'Certainly does,' replied the tall young man, 'Enjoy!'

'Ooh!' teased Catherine, 'Is the young man flirting with you?'

'He has a name you know!' informed Jane, 'He's called Jacob and all those pictures on the walls are his.'

'Wow,' exclaimed Catherine, 'They're so lifelike. Why is he working in here?' Fearing another deep discussion she stopped herself, 'Actually don't answer that!' Instead, Jane and Catherine watched as Anne broke the edge of the tart with a cake fork.

Catherine broke the silence, 'This flaming diet! I would have eaten three of those ten years ago and not even worried about it.'

'I'm just not that hungry,' Jane chipped in.

'You wouldn't be,' joked Catherine, 'You're all loved up with that Martin bloke.'

Jane just smiled; she couldn't deny it. He was a bad boy turned good. And it's much better that way round rather than when a good boy turns bad – she'd had several of those already.

'Talk of the devil,' remarked Anne casually as she spooned the calorific snack into her face.

The door of the coffee shop flew open and Martin stumbled straight into the ladies' table.

'Talk about a dramatic entrance,' chuckled Jane.

'Hi,' said Martin, and then turning to Anne, he added, 'I'm sorry, but I'm worried about Steven. I wanted to get hold of him and see how the old boy is, but I just can't get through on the phone. So I went round your gaff and knocked but there was no answer. He always gets back to me pronto, even if he's driving. I mean, he'll pull over when he can and call me back. And it's never more than about half an hour to wait.'

Anne was clearly rattled by the news, not least because she wasn't aware that Martin even knew their address. She took her mobile phone out of her handbag and selected 'Husband' from her contacts list. Catherine took a hefty swig of coffee as the others sat tensely waiting. The call was clearly connecting as the ring tone could be heard, but after around a dozen iterations Anne decided to cancel the call.

'Not answering,' she stated matter-of-factly, 'What can it mean?'

'Perhaps he's popped out for some fresh air,' suggested Jane.

'No, he's not been outside for weeks. His immune system isn't up to it and he takes medical advice pretty seriously.'

'Asleep?' ventured Catherine.

'No way. Someone dropping a feather would wake him up. There must be something wrong. I'll have to pop home and see. If I don't, I'll worry about it all afternoon.'

'But it's 12.50 already. You'll never walk there and back to work by 1pm,' reasoned Jane.

'I can give you a lift if you like. I'm in the car today,' said Martin, and then thinking twice he turned to Jane, 'If you're comfortable with that of course.'

Jane smiled. She trusted him, and Anne wouldn't abuse the trust of a colleague she'd known for years anyway, she wasn't that kind of person, she did accounts!

'Yeah, no worries. Are we still meeting up tonight?'

'You bet!' grinned Martin.

Catherine winked teasingly at Jane, and before anybody could utter another word Anne had shovelled the lion's share of the fruit tart into her mouth and grabbed her coat from the back of the chair. Swallowing hard she addressed her two colleagues, 'If anyone asks where I am I shouldn't be long. Just say it's a family emergency.'

'Of course,' said Jane, and with that the pair were gone, giving the effect of a whirlwind whipping through the coffee shop. A small brown hatchback awaited and the pair climbed in.

Anne had only spoken to Martin a couple of times when he had come into the coffee shop during lunch to visit Jane, so she felt a little uneasy about travelling in this former drug user's car. She was also puzzled as to why Steven had given Martin his address when they always met at the pub. He had never visited before, at least not while she was there, but there she was being chauffeured to her own abode by a man she hardly knew, and worse still, a man she viewed as playing Russian roulette with her husband's mental health.

'Just out of curiosity,' she ventured, 'Was it something urgent you wanted to speak to him about?'

'Kind of,' said Martin, 'He wanted me to look at this website he goes on but when I tried there was nothing there. I said I'd try again but I kept forgetting to do it, you know, I was meeting Jane and stuff, getting all wrapped up in that. Anyhow, earlier I was thinking about the old boy and I thought I'd try it, to help him out, like. Well, there was nothing there at all, so I played around a bit, with numbers I mean.'

Anne's face registered bewilderment.

'The website is a long number,' explained Martin, 'The gist of it is that if you start at two and you keep doubling in the end you'll reach the figure that leads to this website. Well, I kept on doubling some more and trying all the numbers as web addresses, using the same ending. Nothing, nothing, nothing, and then eventually I got something that freaked me out. It was a screen of funny squares, like 3D bar-code. Well, it panicked me and I shut the browser down straight away; I didn't want to get a virus. I know Steven would want to know about it though cos the first website has been doing his head in, so this'll blow his mind completely. In a good way I mean. I want to try and help him.'

Anne wasn't sure that this was the kind of help that Steven needed, but Martin was assisting her by giving her a lift so she decided to keep her thoughts to herself. 'Well, I guess you know him as well as I do, but he's very fragile mentally. Just take care.'

'Sure thing,' stated Martin, and within a few minutes he was indicating right and parking beneath the magnolia tree, which had now jettisoned most of its pink and white petals onto the ground. 'I'll wait in the car. If you need me I'm here.'

Anne fired the passenger door open and shuffled her keys around in her hand as she walked assertively to the front door. Within seconds she was inside. 'Steven! Steven!' she called, but she was greeted by nothing but silence.

She stormed up the stairs and into the bedroom, 'Are you in?' The bed was empty and neatly made, so she wandered across the landing to the study. 'He'll be on that blasted computer,' she thought.

'Steven!' she called again as she opened the wooden door to the little room. The computer was switched on but there was no Steven to be seen.

She stopped in her tracks. 'What on earth is he looking at?' she muttered, surveying the mass of black and white squares on the screen that looked like a giant QR code. She mused how some women worried that their husbands were secretly viewing pornography online. Trust hers to be secretly viewing some kind of bonkers 'mind trip' instead. 'I wish he'd shut the damn thing down!' she said, clicking on the start menu and selecting *Shut Down*, 'He must realise we're in a *cost of living* crisis!'

The screen went dark, and while this action was saving her a few pennies on the electricity bill, it wasn't solving the mystery of where her sick husband had absconded to. She scratched her head on both sides and tried to rally her thoughts, 'Think! Think!'

Meanwhile outside, Martin gazed down the cosy suburban road in the direction of the moors that overlooked Wickersby. At the end he could see the terraces of houses that crept up the hillside beyond the town centre, with a thick mass of trees above them, and at the top, empty moorland. There was a thin plume of smoke coming from the summit, just to the left of the line of trees that shrouded the A48.

'It must be coming from that church that he was going to,' Martin deduced, 'There's nothing else up there.'

The peace of the moment was shattered by Anne yanking open the car door. 'I don't know what to do,' she panicked, 'He's nowhere to be seen. He's ill. He shouldn't be outside and he's left his phone on the kitchen worktop. We can't contact him and we've got no way of finding out where he is.'

Martin remained calm, and trying to avert his eyes from the rising smoke on the hillside, for fear of panicking Anne further, he asked, 'Do you think he would have popped up to that church again?'

'Jesus! I thought it was only me who knew about that,' scoffed Anne, 'He's been telling the world and his wife about his delusions!'

Martin played it safe, 'I know it sounds weird but I just wondered if he might have gone up there for a bit of a pray.'

'Everything he does is weird these days,' said Anne, 'But the car is still there.'

'Doh!' Martin mocked himself, 'Should've spotted that,'

although in truth he had no idea what Steven's car even looked like as he'd always met him at pubs and he had only been to Steven's house once before, a few hours ago. Steven had given him his address years ago, but until today he'd never had any reason to use it. 'Shall I take you back to work? You'll have to tell me where it is, mind you.'

'We've got to find him,' Anne reasoned, 'He's not well in body or mind. He knows that. Why on earth has he gone out?'

'Do you think he could have got a taxi to the church? I mean, he knows he's not up to driving.'

'He's got to be seriously desperate to go to church if he's booked a taxi,' Anne rebutted, 'But why of all places do you think he'd go there?'

'I dunno really. It just seemed to be an important place to him. He was getting right into religion, but not in a normal way. I don't want to be rude about your husband but he was doing some really strange experiments at that church, like he was trying to trick God or something.'

By now Martin had given the game away as Anne followed his gaze through the windscreen to the plume of smoke that was rising from the hilltop.

'Oh no!' she exclaimed, 'You don't think...?'

'Well, like you say, he wasn't well in body or mind.'

Anne recalled a passage she'd read in one of his little black books about wanting to seal things that he'd said inside Saint Cecilia's and wanting the abhorrent thoughts to never emerge from that building. 'He's gone and set fire to it,' she thought aloud, 'He's trying to burn his own thoughts!'

'What the...?'

'We've got to go up there. I think he's finally lost it!'

And with that Martin turned the key in the ignition and they were off. As the brown hatchback sped through the parked cars on either side of the straight suburban road Anne phoned Catherine and told her that she wouldn't be back for a while and instructed her to apologise to Mr Jessop if he came out of his office and questioned her. 'Family emergency, remember?'

'Got it!' affirmed her colleague.

Before long they were rattling their way up the hill onto the moor. Anne nervously held onto her seatbelt. Martin had metamorphosed into some kind of rally driver and this was a marked contrast to Steven's sedate style of driving which she was used to. Trees and foliage whipped past as she looked out of the side window, concluding that this would be less scary than looking at the road ahead. There was a large goods lorry trundling up the hill and Martin zoomed straight past it on the opposite side of the road.

'Sorry,' he said to Anne as she winced, 'But we're in a hurry, right?'

Anne just nodded and soon the car was screeching into the drive to St Cecilia's. The fact that the smoke was coming from the church was now indisputable, with black clouds billowing from the tower.

'Oh my God! What if he's in there?'

'That's what we're here to find out,' reassured Martin as he spun the car into a parking space and flung open the door.

Martin was halfway up the path to the church's main door before Anne had even extricated herself from the vehicle. He twisted the circular loop of metal and pushed the heavy wooden door. In truth there was no way of opening the door quickly and all the effort that had gone into shoving it seemed to dissipate as it slowly opened. Inside was the second door with the latch. Martin slid it along and pushed again, only to find himself engulfed by smoke, which sent him reeling backwards into Anne, who had just stumbled inside.

'Steven!' he yelled at the top of his voice 'Are you in there?' but all the pair could hear was the cracking of fire eating up wood. Anne choked on the acrid fumes as Martin called out again, 'Steven! It's Martin!' His accomplice then added her own shout to the cacophony, 'It's me, Steven. Come out!'

The billowing smoke seemed to dissipate, returning to its original course of rising directly up through the rafters of the main body of the church, allowing Martin a glimpse of the carnage inside. There was a mass of burning wood in the middle aisle. It seemed as though the fire had been started by somebody smashing up the wooden seats and piling them into an unholy bonfire.

He could make out an upside-down table which had been flipped onto the flaming pile and he imagined the rage that must have possessed Steven to have created this almighty mess. 'I didn't think he had it in him!' he said, as he stood helplessly watching the flames soar upward. He looked at the puny fire extinguisher hanging on the wall by the open door and deduced that trying to use that to put out the fire would be like trying to douse a volcano with a cupful of water. He grabbed it regardless and turned to Anne, who already had her mobile phone in her hand; 'I think we need to make a 999 call.'

And then summoning up all his energy for one last time, he yelled at the top of his voice 'Steeeeveeen!' before spraying the entire contents of the fire extinguisher at the blaze.

It was no good. The smoke was making the pair of them cough and the fire was out of control. The warmth caressed their faces but their lungs protested loudly, so the pair walked outside and closed the outer door, to attempt to contain the fire. Anne had requested the fire brigade and an ambulance, just in case her husband was in there somewhere.

'I'm just going to have a gander round the back,' Martin informed her, 'Are you alright to stay by the car for a minute?'

Anne nodded and Martin began his clockwise perambulation around the outside of the little stone church. As he rounded the corner of the tower he glimpsed the strangest sight. All the bibles and hymn books from within the church had been piled up neatly against the grey stone wall that bounded the graveyard behind the church. Beyond the wall was nothing but moorland – just miles of rolling heather.

"Steven, you loon,' exclaimed Martin under his breath as he stared at the empty moor, 'You didn't have the heart to burn any bibles, did you?'

Just then he could hear the sound of sirens. The emergency services must have been on their way up the hill out of Wickersby, so he rejoined Anne back at the car and together they waited...

Chapter 28 (Steven)

I opened my eyes to find myself in bed. It was a strange bed. Our double bed indoors is made of light-coloured pinewood but this was black-painted metal and the mattress seemed more solid and much higher. The room was strange too. First I noticed that instead of there being spotlights in the ceiling there was a bulbous green glass lampshade that looked like something one would find in an antique shop. And the cupboards were metal too. In fact the room was a different shape. There was an alcove to my right where there should have been a wall.

I looked at my hands and they looked alien to me. The skin was thin and wrinkly with veins protruding like motorways on a map. These were not the hands of a 37-year-old – more like a 73-year-old. And then some! My first thought was that somebody must be playing some kind of mind-trick on me, like one of those psychological illusionists on the TV. What was that bloke's name – Derren somebody? My mind was slow today, but I felt sure that someone was trying to make me think that I was an old man or that I'd been in a coma for forty years and just woken up.

My wife was sleeping peacefully with her head tucked down beneath the quilt. Nothing unusual there, but I thought she'd taken to sleeping in the spare room these days because I'd got that crazy bat virus. It felt as though I'd slipped into a parallel universe, and I got up to investigate. First question: where was I?

The curtains were drawn, but they were long, blue and velvety, not at all like the short linen ones that Anne liked, which were pale with floral designs on them. Perhaps we had travelled to a hotel and I had forgotten that we were away, but where could we be? We never went on holiday any more. All the fun had dried up years ago.

I didn't want to wake Anne, not at least until I'd regained my bearings, so I peeled back a corner of the curtain to look outside.

No, that definitely wasn't Wickersby – not with buildings that size. I was in a city somewhere, and what odd-looking cars they had here – tiny little things, all electric. I let the curtain fall back and the darkness washed back across the room. Anne was still fast asleep and I noticed that there was a bathroom adjoining the bedroom, so I silently shuffled into it, wiping the sleep from my eyes and turning on the tap. I splashed my face with some warm water and pulled a towel from the rail to dry myself, again barely focusing on anything.

As I rubbed the soft brown towel across my face I caught a glimpse of some grey hair in the mirror and slowly I lowered it to reveal my own features but weathered by time and adorned with a shocked expression. My hair was grey – completely grey – and I had heavy lines across my forehead. My skin looked thin and mottled; I looked about eighty!

You can come out now, the game's up, I know this is a trick!

Then I thought, was I stuck in a dream? How many times had I dreamed lucidly and tried to wake myself up upon realising that I was asleep, only to find it nigh on impossible? I felt my eyes with my fingers. They were definitely open. This action wasn't really logical anyway, because if I was really dreaming I wouldn't be able to feel if my eyes were closed in the real world, but I was confused and I'd tried that before in lucid dreams. But this felt real, one hundred percent. When you're in a dream you usually believe it completely, but when you're awake you realise that reality feels completely different. It's amazing that we don't rumble that we're dreaming every time.

I looked down to find that I was wearing grey pyjamas that felt silky to the touch. Since when had I taken to wearing posh stuff like that? I usually wear the T-shirt-style pyjamas, but this was something you'd expect Mr Darcy to be wearing in a TV adaptation of 'Pride and Prejudice.'

I climbed back into bed. Anne was facing outwards, so I could only see the top of her head which was buried into the quilt. She must have dyed her hair as it looked much darker than usual, and she was wearing a pink silky nightdress. How odd. She usually wore the plainest looking nightwear you could ever imagine. I lifted the cover up, taking care not to wake her, but I couldn't deduce much about her appearance with her head snuggled deep into the bed.

Just then her breathing pattern changed with a sudden intake of air and she flopped towards me onto her back. This wasn't Anne at all! I gasped with the shock of it and covered my mouth. What on earth was I doing? Was I having an affair? Why couldn't I remember where I was ? And why did I look so old? I gazed across the woman's face like a rock-climber peering over the top of a summit he'd just reached.

The features looked familiar, very familiar indeed. She didn't look as old as I did, perhaps in her late fifties but it was the nose that I recognised. It was very straight and it reminded me of a ski-slope.

I'd seen that nose before, on Anabelle at the pub, but this *wasn't* Anabelle, this woman looked old enough to be Anabelle's grandmother. Well, just about. I'd never been into all that 'older woman' stuff so had I gone barking mad? But then I thought, I was even older than the lady in the pink nightdress if we were going purely on appearance.

'This isn't fun any more. It would make great TV, I'm sure, but I've had enough. Who wants to watch a confused 37-year-old looking across the face of a sixty-year-old woman that looks like a young barmaid from the Unicorn after doing forty more circuits around the sun? This has got to be a hoax. It's amazing what they can do with prosthetics. I bet we've both been heavily made up in some way – the lengths they go to to make these tricks work!'

I scratched around at my hands. Maybe the thin aging skin was stuck on. Ouch – that really hurt!

I felt around my neck and chin too. Perhaps the facial prosthetics would pull off easier, but there was nothing to yank at. The make-up department had clearly done an excellent job for whatever magician had pulled this trick on me. And Anabelle must have been in on the trick, but how the hell did they get Anne to agree to this?

The old version of Anabelle had fallen back asleep again. I couldn't just lay there, sleep was clearly history for me tonight, so I got back up. There were some check-patterned slippers by the side of the bed and a dark blue dressing gown hanging over a peg on the bathroom door. The slippers were a comfortable fit as was the dressing gown. They research everything for these tricks right down to your shoe size.

Outside of the room was a short corridor with a window along the outer wall. This was covered by net curtains. I could see the bright lights of whatever city I was in once again, and tall surreal-looking blocks behind the older-looking residential buildings. We weren't very high up, so I deduced that we were in a similar residence. But what about those funny cars? Perhaps I was abroad. They drive different cars in some countries, don't they? I bet there's dozens of countries that are ahead of the UK when it comes to transitioning to electric cars.

There was a picture hanging on the wall opposite the window. My mouth fell open. 'What the hell...?' I quietly muttered to myself. I leaned in closer. My eyesight wasn't great and this in itself was weird – I could read the small print on the beer pumps from the door of the Unicorn. Now, this must have been some kind of fake wedding picture, as it showed me in a dark brown suit marrying Anabelle from the pub. Wow – she looks amazing in that wedding dress!

I just stood staring at it, transfixed, and then at last some memories began to flood into my mind. I *did* marry Anabelle, didn't I? When I had long COVID or whatever it was, Anne and I started sleeping in separate rooms, but when I recovered things never went back to how they were before. We grew further and further apart and in the end we divorced. After running over and over what Anabelle had said on the night she split up with her boyfriend I thought 'What the hell, I've got nothing to lose!' so I asked her if she was still interested in seeing me, and she said that she was. We went to that Japanese restaurant that had just opened in Wickersby. It was funny, as she'd never used chop sticks before and she ended up with rice all over the floor. In the end the manager just brought her a knife and fork. I thought we were just going out as friends, but when I went to kiss her goodnight on the cheek, she somehow moved and things became passionate. Serendipity, I guess.

It was very nice after years of my marriage being as dried up as the bed of a river that has since changed its course. I was still alive; I hadn't died inside, and I'd thought for a long time that I had. The dates with Anabelle became regular after that, and after a year or so I proposed. Anne had moved back to her parents' place by then and the bills for our house were sky-high, so Anabelle suggested moving in straight away and sharing the costs. She'd never left her parents' house before, so it was all new and exciting for her, and even though I was about 39 then, the excitement was contagious and I felt younger than I had felt before.

And then came the marriage, but this time we didn't hold the service in Saint Cecilia's Church. That place, lovely though it was, held dark memories for me. Instead, we had a registry office ceremony and I remember waking that morning and wondering if I'd made the right decision. That day Wickersby was shrouded in mist, like it had been on that day when I gazed across it from Saint Cecilia's. It seemed a bad omen, but by the time of our slot it was merely dull and drizzly, so the rather pedestrian location didn't seem to matter in the end.

People said that it wouldn't work with us having a fifteen-year age gap, but it did, so more fool them. We didn't argue like I did with Anne either. Although Anabelle was younger than Anne, she seemed much more skilled when it came to diplomacy, perhaps it was working in bars that had made her that way. Anne was very practical and Annabelle was more of a dreamer. Somehow, it just worked and the sense of calm helped my *dissociation* issues no end.

That said, I was right in a way about the romance fading after time, but this time around it didn't feel as though I had been cheated. Because things were much more easygoing there was no reason to separate. The arrangement worked for us both financially and also in terms of friendship, but how long had we been together?

Of course, there was the party – our ruby wedding anniversary. So that would make me 79 and Anabelle 64.

Memories kept flooding in as though some kind of fog was clearing. I knew we were having another party for my eightieth birthday next year – a nineties party. I bet hardly anyone else there will remember all the music we've asked the DJ to play – Oasis, Blur, R.E.M., maybe even a bit of jungle or rave. They were good days for music. It always seemed like the last time there was anything original before the money men shaped every aspect of culture in the pursuit of maximum profit. Anabelle doesn't share my view, so it's especially nice that she's organised this party for me and she's promised not to inflict all that awful 2020s stuff on us all. Yes, she obviously still has a lot of affection for me after all these years to pay attention to small details like this.

It was beginning to feel as though I was waking up from a dream. This was a dream where I had been a young man, lost in confusion, but it was all so simple now. I had no further goals to achieve, so it didn't matter what anyone thought about me. I used to hate all that judging that went on. Just because I worked in a bar they were constantly telling me that I should be doing something mind-sapping and soul-destroying just to get more money. But in old age we all end up the same, so more fool them for spending so long doing things they don't like. I'd been retired for a dozen years now, and I was enjoying it. The great thing is, once you no longer worry about what people think of you or about your choices, that whole *impostor syndrome* thing goes away, or at least recedes to a tolerable level.

We'd moved southward to Chatford a while ago. It was somewhere we'd been for a seaside break when I retired and the flat that I was now standing in came up at a good price so we thought 'why not?' It was weird being right in the centre of a city near all the office blocks, but it was very handy to be close to the shops and the railway station now that we were getting on a bit. They've got some amazing trains these days, although it's still quite a mission to get back up to Wickersby to revisit old haunts, not that I go there very often these days.

The other plus point was that our flat had no stairs. I can still get up and down steps at the moment but it's not going to be like this forever, is it? You've always got to think ahead! Yes, that's where I was, in our flat. How did I forget that? I must have been half asleep.

I decided to pull my gaze away from that old wedding photo and continue through the short corridor to the living room. I already knew it was the living room as my memory was firing on all cylinders now. Yes, the art deco settee and furniture. Anne would have never had anything like that in the house, but Anabelle was much more open-minded and we'd made all those choices together. Really, I wasn't even conscious that we were making choices; it was all so flipping easy!

The computer on the desk was still flashing a green light, although the monitor had shut down. This was unusual as I normally always turn it off before going to bed. The screens are so thin these days that it seems like a miracle to me how they get all the technology inside. That said, you can't really shrink the keyboard as human hands are the same size as they have always been. Technology can't change everything!

I placed my index finger onto the touch screen and an image appeared. Yes, that's what I'd been looking at – that weird website they'd been talking about on the news – two to the power of thirty. It's a weird thing that lets you send messages back to your younger self. Well, it does and it doesn't. Only certain types of info can get through. Most of what you try to type in gets rejected but occasionally you can get something past the technology. I had just told my younger self to pray for the opposite of whatever he wants. You see, I didn't believe in anything beyond the here and now back then, which is fair enough I suppose, but I remember how dry life seemed when my first marriage was splitting up and I thought a little bit of mystery might add some colour for him, I mean me.

I've been reverse-praying ever since that day, and although it doesn't always work it's my little twist on faith, and who's to say that it's wrong if it doesn't harm anyone? I don't really believe in it but I do it all the same. You could say that I've partitioned my mind like a computer. There's one operating system where belief is part of the program and another where it isn't. So how did I convince my younger self to try reverse-praying the first place?

I made up some mumbo-jumbo about scientists having done lots of tests which prove that it works so that my younger self would at least give it a try. I mean, it's not really deception, is it? I just wanted my younger self to listen, and if you can't have a joke with yourself who can you have a joke with? OK, it might have been in poor taste to tell him to pray for his own death to come early, but look at the facts, I'm 79 and I'm still here, so it didn't do any harm. I think that cancer scare I had a few years ago was on my mind. I just wanted to make sure it wouldn't come back, and although reverse-praying is illogical and just my own superstition really, I thought I had nothing to lose.

I've still got some of those old diaries that I wrote around that time so I used a few entries to prove that I was really him, but older. It seems that they only get through if he'd already written them at the time he read the email. It was bonkers, but I knew those old diaries would come in handy one day.

Oddly enough, I stopped writing them when I discovered the '1,073,741,824' website. I used to receive the messages on a website that was 'two to the power of twenty' but once I discovered the 'two to the power of thirty' website, life seemed to fly by in a flash. Well, that makes me wonder, did I just travel from there to here instantly – from 'Steven Jones aged 37' to 'Steven Jones aged 79?' The memories are all there, but it seems odd how I perceive them. It's as though my entire life was just a dream. It's there, but it's not vivid at all.

So, let's hypothesise that the connection between now and back then actually does create some kind of portal that my consciousness just travelled through, the fact that I can remember everything that happened in between, however vaguely, doesn't mean that I didn't experience those things, does it? I feel old, after all. I don't feel like a 37-year-old; I feel 79. Look, I can't touch my toes any more. Ouch – I won't try that again!

The technology we've got these days is amazing. Who'd have thought you could send messages across the decades via a website which transmits them using gravity waves? I don't think we even know the effects of what we're doing at all. It's always the same with technology – we bang it out there and deal with the consequences afterwards.

Well it's 3.06am, so I really should go back to bed. I feel more able to sleep now.

I wander back through the short corridor, passing the wedding picture, I remove my dressing gown and slippers and I gently climb back beneath the quilt. Anabelle sleeps like a log; it's hard to wake her really. I lie there and stare up at the green glass lampshade again. The bulbous shape casts a long shadow across the ceiling, and it reminds me of the way that those younger years cast a long shadow across the rest of your life.

It's been a good life all in all, but I don't imagine that I have many decades left now. Life expectancy hasn't increased dramatically beyond what it was when I was young. If you reach ninety you're doing well, and if you reach a hundred people still treat you like a legend. The world record for age has crept up to 124, but I don't think I'm going to make that. I've sampled too many real ales! Being a record breaker and reaching 128 would be good, of course, as nobody has yet reached 'two to the power of seven.'

It seems as though I've had two lives; one that seemed to pass quite slowly when I was young, growing up and then marrying Anne, and then there's this second life which seems to have passed by in a flash, in an instant even.

Let's humour the idea and imagine that my consciousness really did whiz forward 42 years in the instant that I logged onto that website as a young man, just how would it have seemed to those left behind who knew me at the time? Would I have carried on going through the motions of my life – divorcing Anne, marrying Anabelle, moving to Chatford, etc. without even being conscious at the time? Or would I have just disappeared altogether, reappearing in a universe where all those things had already happened? Perhaps the old version of me is still stuck in the past getting more and more crazy with every visit to Saint Cecilia's. He'll have probably torched the place by now!

Sometimes you can think too much.

But what can I say? How can I summarise the two experiences – 37 years that I seemed to feel deeply, and another 42 that I have memories of but feel as though I never truly experienced?

I turn to gaze at Anabelle, as she breathes rhythmically, out, in, out, in, making the quilt rise and fall each time. Her face looks smooth and her expression is relaxed. She is blissfully unaware of all of this.

Yes, what can I say?

Is it better to live life being blissfully unaware, or to analyse everything but find no answers?

I turn back and look at the shadow from the lampshade again.

All I can really say is 'I have lived!'

About Adam Colton

Born in 1975, Adam Colton is a writer of humorous travelogues, music reviews and psychological fiction from Kent, UK. His first paperback documented an attempt to visit every lighthouse on the mainland coast of England and Wales undertaken with his father, Roger Colton, who published and contributed to the book which was featured on the BBC news to mark National Lighthouse Day and became the subject of a question on the quiz show, University Challenge.

Since then, Adam has straddled the line between documenting his lightly philosophical UK travel escapades and mind-blowing fiction. One of his short stories was short-listed for the HG Wells festival's short story competition. He is also a writer of topical songs, performing as one half of the duo Adam and Teresa, whose song 'Fat Cats with a Death Wish on the M25' received airplay on BBC Radio Kent.

If you have enjoyed this book please review it on your favourite online bookstore. Details of other books by Adam Colton are listed below.

NON-FICTION:

England and Wales in a Flash (father and son jaunt around the mainland coast in search of every lighthouse)

Mud, Sweat and Beers (two friends hike across Southern England from Kent to Somerset between two villages of the same name documenting their adventure)

Bordering on Lunacy (father and son explore the lighthouses of Southern Scotland and trace the route of the border with England)

Stair-Rods and Stars (enjoy the positive vibes as our roaming cyclist relishes the rail trails, ale trails, ridgeways and waterways of Southern England)

2021: A Musical Odyssey (poring over the classic rock albums that grace the author's extensive collection, memories spark and humour abounds in this personal guide which reflects upon the importance of music in all our lives – file under 'rock and droll')

FICTION:

Conundrum - 'Seven Dreams of Reality' and 'The Kent-erbury Tales' (surreal short stories, often set at iconic Kentish locations, with dark twists and dystopian undertones)

Codename: Narcissus (in Adam Colton's first novel, Tim is a cold controller, his wife is slowly losing it and his new best friend is you!)

The Dream Machine (Labyrinth of Dreams) (there's no escape from technology – even while you're sleeping. The 'Conundrum' stories about a dream recording machine form the basis of a novella)

The Nightshade Project (Donna is an ordinary teenager, but with a silicon chip brain implant as her eighteenth birthday present, is it Donna who is coming of age or the entire world?)

Printed in Great Britain
by Amazon